I0703421

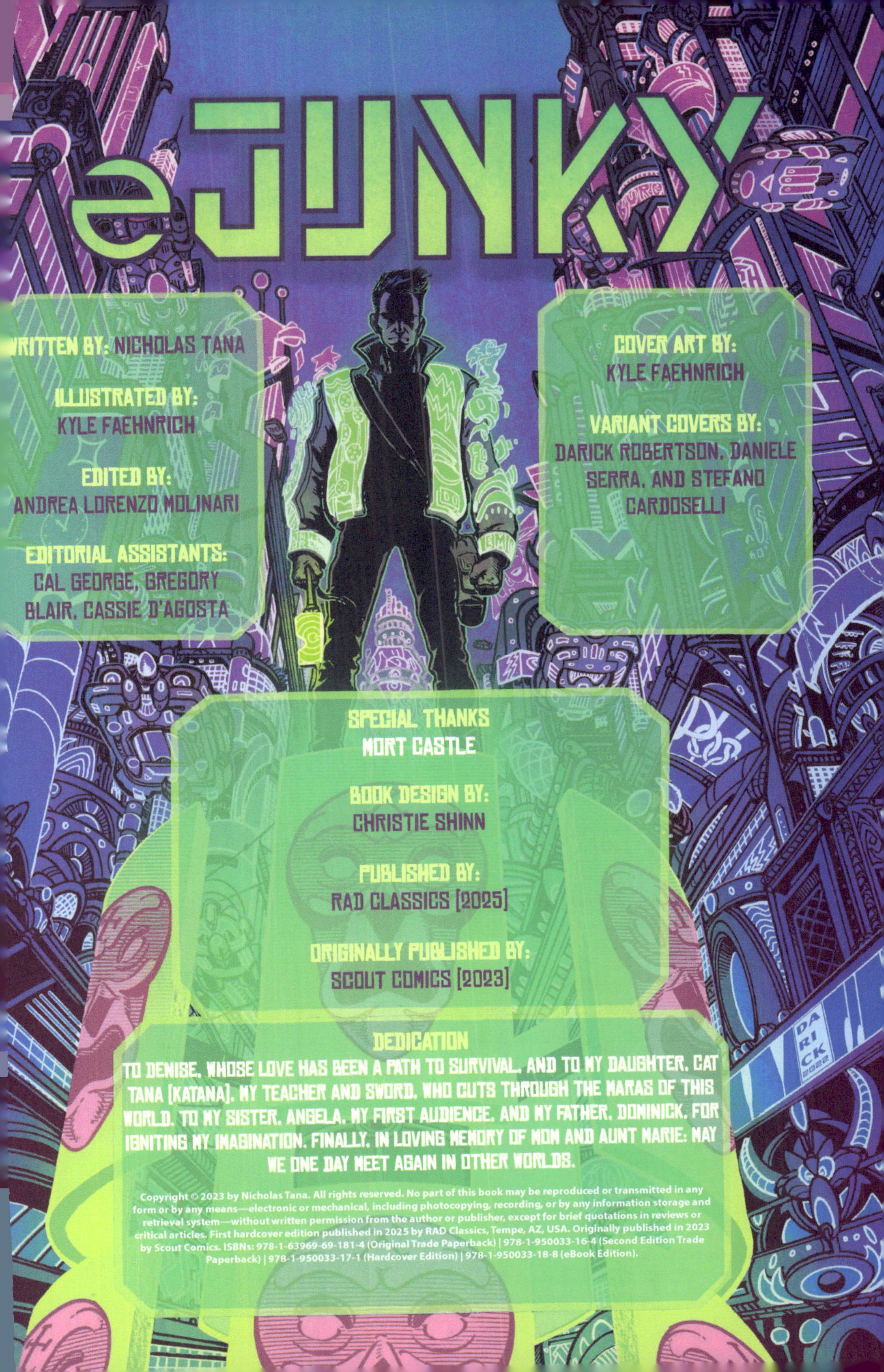

eJUNKY

WRITTEN BY: NICHOLAS TANA

ILLUSTRATED BY:
KYLE FAEHNRICH

EDITED BY:
ANDREA LORENZO MOLINARI

EDITORIAL ASSISTANTS:
CAL GEORGE, GREGORY
BLAIR, CASSIE D'AGOSTA

COVER ART BY:
KYLE FAEHNRICH

VARIANT COVERS BY:
DARICK ROBERTSON, DANIELE
SERRA, AND STEFANO
CARDOSELLI

SPECIAL THANKS
MORT CASTLE

BOOK DESIGN BY:
CHRISTIE SHINN

PUBLISHED BY:
RAD CLASSICS (2025)

ORIGINALLY PUBLISHED BY:
SCOUT COMICS (2023)

DEDICATION
TO DENISE, WHOSE LOVE HAS BEEN A PATH TO SURVIVAL, AND TO MY DAUGHTER, CAT
TANA (KATANA), MY TEACHER AND SWORD, WHO CUTS THROUGH THE MARAS OF THIS
WORLD, TO MY SISTER, ANGELA, MY FIRST AUDIENCE, AND MY FATHER, DOMINICK, FOR
IGNITING MY IMAGINATION. FINALLY, IN LOVING MEMORY OF MOM AND AUNT MARIE: MAY
WE ONE DAY MEET AGAIN IN OTHER WORLDS.

1
THE GUARDIANS OF PAIN

YAMUT KAFIR!
...PAIN...
...EVEN DEATH.
THOUGH THE FRUIT OF EXPERIENCE IS TASTY...
...TO LIVE A THOUSAND LIVES HAS CONSEQUENCES...

...AND THE DREAM...
...BECOMES A NIGHTMARE.

IN SPITE OF IT...
HUFF
HUFF
HUFF
THMP
SIGH
GOOD EVENING MR. HOLMES
...WE STILL WANT MORE.

YANK
SIGH
CLICK
CLICK
BONK
BINK

POP
YAWN
EMO REG
GUARANTEED TO MAKE YOU HAPPY
REGULATE YOUR EMOTIONS 24/7
WHILE MOST PEOPLE ACCEPT MANUFACTURED BLISS...
...THROUGH EMOTIONAL REGULATION...

...AN eJUNKY MUST EXPERIENCE IT ALL...
RESTRICTED ZONE
NEIGHBORHOOD ENCAMPMENT.
ACCESS PROHIBITED
...NO MATTER THE COST.
HECTOR HOLMES AGE 36
SUB-ALTERNATIVE REALITY INVESTIGATION SQUAD
STATUS: RETIRED
YOUR BADGE IS EXPIRED. YOU SHOULDN'T BE HERE.
YOU MUST BE NEW. SAM WON'T BE HAPPY.

WHAT'S ALL THE EXCITEMENT ABOUT?
COME ON, MATRIX!
WHAT'S SO BIG THAT SAMMY CAN'T LET IN HIS NUMBER ONE CUSTOMER?
I NEED A DOSE. MY MIND'S GONE MUSH.
BOSS'S GOT A BIG MEETING WITH A NEW SUPPLIER.
I'LL BE IN AND OUT BEFORE YOU KNOW IT.
BE QUICK ABOUT IT!

STEP CLOSER.
I CAN'T SEE YOU.

WHY DON'T YOU GUARDIANS
SHOW YOUR FACE?

WE PREFER THE
MYSTERY OF THEATER.

BESIDES...

...WHAT WE'RE
DEALING IS
ILLEGAL.

CAN'T GET MORE ILLEGAL THAN US.
NOT THE SAME.
WHAT WE'VE GOT WILL START A REVOLUTION.
PROVE IT!
WHIRR
SSSSSSS
KER-CHK
TWITCH

CRASH
BLAMM
EEEYAAH!
AAIIIEEEE!
AAHHH!
YYAAGH!
UUUGHH.
WHAT HAPPENED?!
AAAAAA!
DON'T KNOW!

EVEN IF I DID KNOW, IT'S BETTER TO...
...SAY NOTHING...
...GET OUT FAST!

AND NOW...
...THE SHOW YOU'VE ALL BEEN WAITING FOR...
...ASTRA'S HOLOGRAM PROJECTION OF HER LATEST DREAM, PERFORMING NOW AT HEAVEN'S HALL.
COURTESY OF THE W.C.O., YOUR WORLD CORPORATION ORGANIZATION!
STREAMED LIVE FOR ALL TO SEE!
I'M ASTRA.
WELCOME TO MY DREAM.
COURTESY OF THE WCO
WORLD CORPORATION ORGANIZATION
HEAVEN'S HALL

THEY LOVE HER DREAMS SO MUCH...
...THEY'VE FORGOTTEN THEIR OWN.

RUIIPP
MMMmm!
BZZZTTT
BZZZZZ
WAKE!
WAKE!
WAKE!

THIS IS X OF THE GUARDIANS OF PAIN.
WE'RE INTERRUPTING THIS BROADCAST TO BRING YOU THIS LIFE-SAVING MESSAGE.
THE W.C.O. HAS ERASED YOUR SUFFERING BY TAKING CONTROL OF YOUR THOUGHTS AND EMOTIONS.
REPLACING DEMOCRACY WITH CORPORATOCRACY!
DISTRACTING YOU WITH ADVERTISEMENTS AND GAMES... WHILE YOU WASTE YOUR LIVES AWAY WATCHING OTHERS' DREAMS!
LIVING EVERY EXPERIENCE BUT YOUR OWN!
WHAT THE HELL IS THIS?
MUST BE A HACK. KILL THE BROADCAST!
I CAN'T!
CLICK
NO CONTROL!
WE'RE HERE TO BRING YOU THOSE LOST EXPERIENCES THEY'VE STOLEN.
RESTORE THE FORGOTTEN HISTORY THEY'VE ERASED.
BEFORE THE FLAMES OF YOUR ENLIGHTENMENT...
...ARE EXTINGUISHED!
KER-FSSSH

MEANWHILE...
...SAFE AT HOME, ASTRA WAKES.
YEEAAHH!
Ahhh...
IT'S ALL RIGHT.
YOU HAD A BAD DREAM.

YANK
YOU IDIOTS!
DON'T YOU SEE?!
HEY!
YOU CRACKED MY EMO-REG, MAN!
HUH?
LOOK!

ON THE OTHER SIDE OF TOWN...
WE'VE GOT DREAM RECORDINGS OF EVERY TYPE--
--ROCK STAR DREAMS,
PORN STAR DREAMS,
YOU NAME IT.
DREAM PALACE
AND ALTS! WE'VE GOT EVERY ALTERNATIVE EXPERIENCE UNDER THE SUN,
FROM THE RED CARPET, TO GOING OVER NIAGARA FALLS IN A BARREL!
WHAT ABOUT VIRTUAL REALITY?
VIRTS? YEAH, WE GOT VIRTS.
SO OLD SCHOOL.
LOOK, WHY DON'T YOU HOP IN A HOVERCRAFT, AND CHECK US OUT.
RIGHT NOW, I'VE GOT A REAL CUSTOMER.
HECTOR HOLMES, MY MAIN MAZER!

DID YOU SEE HEAVEN'S HALL IS BLAZING?
SURPRISED THEY'D BROADCAST IT FOR SO LONG. THOUGHT THEY'D CUT THE SIGNAL.
@DREAM HACK!
FEELING IS HEALING
AND TO THINK THE W.C.O. WANTS TO PASS A LAW MANDATING THAT WE WEAR THOSE THINGS 24/7.
YOU ALRIGHT?
WELL, BRAIN'S MUSH. OTHERWISE, LIFE'S GOOD.
HA!
WELL, YOU KNOW THE TRADE OFF: THE MORE YOU EXPERIENCE, THE LESS YOU REMEMBER.
MEMORIAL DAY SALE 30% OFF
PARADISE LOST STUDIOS PRESENT
WHAT ARE YOU SO DOSED ABOUT?
WELL, BUSINESS IS BOOMING.
AFTER THAT DREAM HACK, eJUNKIES WILL BE BEGGING FOR WHAT THOSE GUARDIANS ARE PEDDLING.
I'D LIKE TO TRY SOME.
ANYTHING TO ESCAPE, HUH? EVEN IF IT HURTS?
THE MORE IT HURTS, THE BETTER. FEELING SOMETHING'S BETTER THAN FEELING NOTHING.
WELL, YOU'VE COME TO THE RIGHT PLACE.

THEY'RE CALLING IT TORCH.
THIS ALT'S FROM CELLMEM THAT'S CENTURIES OLD.
LOOK HOW IT SHINES!
IMPOSSIBLE. CELLMEM ERODES AFTER A MONTH.
SUPPOSEDLY SCRAPED FROM THE DNA, SO THE EXPERIENCE GETS PRESERVED.
THIS ONE'S FROM A 19TH CENTURY TRAIN WRECK CALLED THE "FAT NANCY."
I WAS HOPING YOU'D DOSE IT FOR ME. AS A FORMER A.R.I.S, YOU CAN HELP AUTHENTICATE IT.
SURE, FOR 2,000 BIT.
WHO YOU KIDDING? YOU LIVE FOR THIS!
I LIVE FOR MYSELF.
ALL RIGHT, 1,000 BIT.
DON'T YOU FEEL LIKE A SELLOUT WEARING THAT CRAP?
JUST GIVE ME THE DOSE, WILL YA?
OH, IT'S COMING. THIS TRAIN'S LEAVING THE STATION!

ORANGE, VIRGINIA.
JULY 12, 1888.
TRAIN 52 CROSSES THE
FORTY-FOUR-FOOT TRESTLE.
WHERE ARE WE?
COMING UP ON THE TRESTLE, DEAR.
HEY! GIVE ME MY MIRROR!
THIS REALLY IS THE 19TH CENTURY!
WHY ARE YOU STARING LIKE THAT, CORNELIUS?
MY GOD! SHE LOOKS JUST LIKE...
WHAT'S THE MATTER?
YOU ALRIGHT, MISTER?

SKREEEEEEEE
CRRAASH
OH GOD!
SAVE ME!

AAHHHH HHHH
HUFF HUFF
TAKE IT EASY!
W-WHERE AM I?
SUN VALLEY HOSPITAL. I'VE NOTIFIED THE DOCTOR YOU'RE AWAKE.
TRY TO RELAX, MR. HOLMES. YOU'VE BEEN IN A COMA FOR FIFTY-THREE HOURS.
KNOCK KNOCK
A.R.I.S.
ALTERNATIVE REALITY INVESTIGATION SQUAD
I NEED A FEW MINUTES WITH THE PATIENT.
ALONE?

NOW, WE CAN HAVE A REAL CONVERSATION.
IF YOU WANT TO KILL YOURSELF, MIGHT AS WELL SERVE YOUR COMMUNITY DOING IT.
YOU RETIRED ME, MIKE. REMEMBER? OR IS A.R.I.S. CHANGING ITS POLICY ON eJUNKIES?
NOT OFFICIALLY. BUT UNOFFICIALLY, I COULD USE YOUR SKILLS.
YOU SURVIVED TORCH. THE GUARDIANS' NEW ALT DOSE.
NOBODY ELSE WHO TRIED THIS LATEST BATCH DID.
I GUESS THAT MEANS I'M SPECIAL.
DEFINE SPECIAL.
SO... WHAT WERE YOU DOING IN THE RESTRICTED ZONE?
HOW'D YOU KNOW?
WE TRACED YOUR AD APPAREL.

I MUST HAVE GOTTEN LOST.
WHY? YOU HERE TO ARREST ME?
LOOK, IF I WANTED TO ARREST YOU, I WOULD'VE DONE IT ALREADY.
DID YOU SEE WHO SHOT SAM?
NO. THEY USED A SMOKE BOMB. IS HE ALIVE?
IF YOU CALL BEING A VEGETABLE ALIVE. DO YOU THINK IF YOU DOSED SAM'S CELLMEM, YOU COULD SEE WHAT HAPPENED?
MAYBE. WHY DON'T YOU DOSE IT?
TOO RISKY. TOO ADDICTIVE. BUT THAT NEVER STOPPED YOU.
THERE'S SOMETHING ELSE I THINK YOU SHOULD KNOW THAT MIGHT MOTIVATE YOU TO HELP US.
I'M LISTENING.
YOUR BROTHER ALEX WAS INVESTIGATING THE GUARDIANS AROUND THE TIME HE DIED. TO MAKE THINGS MORE COMPLICATED, HE THOUGHT HIS WIFE WAS HAVING AN AFFAIR WITH ONE OF THEM.
TO BE HONEST, IF YOU HADN'T WITNESSED ALEX'S DEATH, I WOULD'VE SUSPECTED THE GUARDIANS OF KILLING HIM.
HE WAS GETTING CLOSE TO IDENTIFYING THEIR LEADER AND STOPPING THEM.
I ASSUME YOU REPORTED THIS TO ARTEMIS?

OF COURSE.
BUT SHE TOLD ME TO BURY IT. AT THE TIME, THE W.C.O. DIDN'T SEE THE GUARDIANS AS A THREAT. SURE, THEY WERE DEALING ILLEGAL ALTS! BUT SO WERE A LOT OF PEOPLE.
THE W.C.O. COULDN'T HAVE CARED LESS WHEN IT WAS LIMITED TO THE RESTRICTED ZONE. THE RECENT DREAM CELEBRITY HACK MADE THEM CHANGE THEIR TUNE.
WHY ARE YOU TELLING ME THIS NOW?
I THOUGHT IT MIGHT INSPIRE YOU TO FINISH WHAT ALEX STARTED. BE A HERO FOR ONCE. LIKE YOUR BROTHER.
I'M NOTHING LIKE MY BROTHER.
AND I DON'T BELIEVE IN HEROES.
WELL, IF YOU CHANGE YOUR MIND.
YOU KNOW WHERE TO FIND ME.
SIGH
A FEW DAYS LATER...
...BACK AT HOME.

BREAKING NEWS
ASTRA HACKED BY DREAM TERRORISTS
THE W.C.O. IS DECLARING WAR ON THE GUARDIANS OF PAIN, AFTER A HACK ON ONE OF ASTRA'S DREAM PROJECTIONS COINCIDED WITH THE BURNING OF HEAVEN'S HALL.
THE PEOPLE AGAINST TECHNOLOGY, ALSO KNOWN AS THE P.A.T....
...HAVE DENIED ANY AFFILIATION WITH THE GUARDIANS.
WE BRING YOU LIVE TO THIS DEBATE...
STR8 TALK
EMO-REGS REGULATE EMOTIONS.
THE VISORS TRACK AND REMOVE PAINFUL STIMULI BEFORE YOU EVER SEE THEM AGAIN.
COLORS DISPLAY MOOD TO HELP US BE MORE SENSITIVE.
HATE CRIMES, DOMESTIC ABUSE, AND SEXUAL HARASSMENT HAVE ALL BEEN VIRTUALLY ELIMINATED IN DISTRICTS WHERE EMO-REGS ARE WORN.
AT WHAT COST?!
GIDEON MARS, W.C.O.
HORUS KHALED, P.A.T.

THE W.C.O. HAS ALREADY TURNED SO MANY OF US INTO eJUNKIES.
I BET IF PEOPLE UNDERSTOOD HOW THOSE THINGS REALLY WORKED--
IT'S NO SECRET.
BIO-INDICATORS DETERMINE EMOTIONAL STATE.
SUBCUTANEOUS NEEDLES INJECT DOPAMINE AND SEROTONIN AS NEEDED--
TELL THAT TO THE PEOPLE WHO BURNED ALIVE IN HEAVEN'S HALL!
WE DON'T NEED A MACHINE CONTROLLING HOW WE FEEL!
WELL, ONE THING'S FOR SURE...
...IF HORUS WAS WEARING AN EMO-REG RIGHT NOW, IT'D BE FLASHING RED! HA HA HA HA HA HA!
FWIP

ACCESS MY BROTHER'S FILE!
FWIP
A.R.I.S. AGENT ALEX HOLMES DIES OF APPARENT SUICIDE AFTER LEAPING OFF BUILDING
DESIRAE.
THAT GIRL ON THE TRAIN...
...LOOKED JUST LIKE HER.

TO BE CONTINUED...

AD APPAREL

DISPLAY YOUR FAVORITE BRAND EXPERIENCES WHILE EARNING BITS FOR EVERYONE WHO VIEWS YOUR ADS. OUR I.E.T.S. (INSEEM EYE TRACKING SENSORS) WILL TRACK EYEBALLS AND AWARD YOU POINTS FOR EVERYONE WHO SEES ANY ADVERTISEMENT YOU DISPLAY.

SUPPLEMENT YOUR W.C.O. STIPEND--EVEN WHILE YOU WORK--WITH ADDED VIEWS! PURCHASES MADE DIRECTLY FROM YOUR EXPERIENCES WILL BE TRACKED AND REWARDED WITH AUTOMATIC UPLOADS OF BITS DEPOSITED DIRECTLY INTO YOUR ACCOUNT. GET YOUR AD APPAREL TODAY!

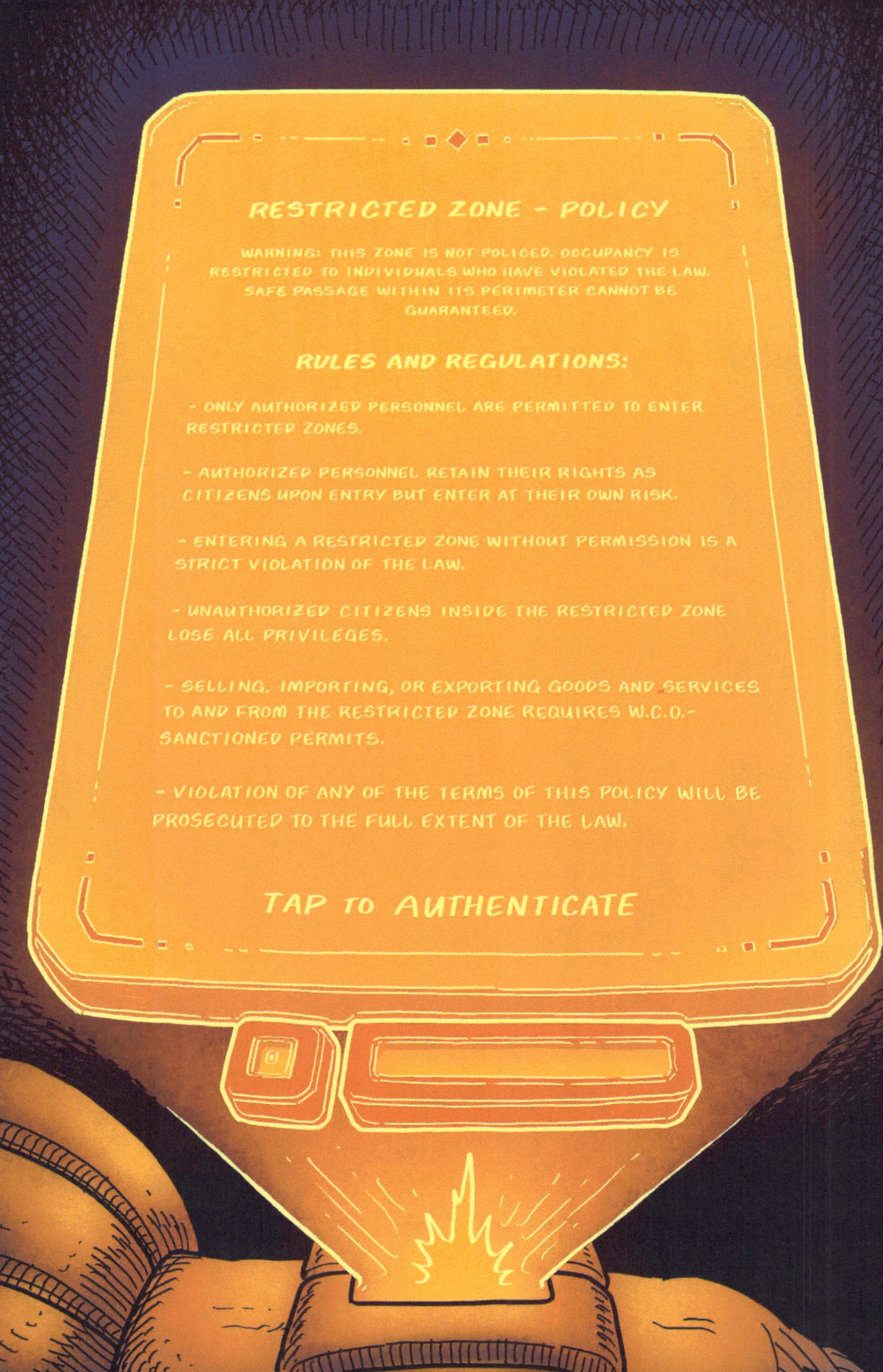

RESTRICTED ZONE - POLICY

WARNING: THIS ZONE IS NOT POLICED. OCCUPANCY IS RESTRICTED TO INDIVIDUALS WHO HAVE VIOLATED THE LAW. SAFE PASSAGE WITHIN ITS PERIMETER CANNOT BE GUARANTEED.

RULES AND REGULATIONS:

- ONLY AUTHORIZED PERSONNEL ARE PERMITTED TO ENTER RESTRICTED ZONES.

- AUTHORIZED PERSONNEL RETAIN THEIR RIGHTS AS CITIZENS UPON ENTRY BUT ENTER AT THEIR OWN RISK.

- ENTERING A RESTRICTED ZONE WITHOUT PERMISSION IS A STRICT VIOLATION OF THE LAW.

- UNAUTHORIZED CITIZENS INSIDE THE RESTRICTED ZONE LOSE ALL PRIVILEGES.

- SELLING, IMPORTING, OR EXPORTING GOODS AND SERVICES TO AND FROM THE RESTRICTED ZONE REQUIRES W.C.O.- SANCTIONED PERMITS.

- VIOLATION OF ANY OF THE TERMS OF THIS POLICY WILL BE PROSECUTED TO THE FULL EXTENT OF THE LAW.

TAP TO AUTHENTICATE

"There is a war happening in Restricted Zone 69 and most every other Zonie alive today is clueless!" says Coco Trenchent, longtime resident of Restricted Zone 69. As the sister of Sam Trenchent, former leader of the most powerful gangs in the territory, she should know.

Violence in Restricted Zones is no surprise. The W.C.O. established Restricted Zones in 2032 as one of their first mandates, giving all criminals, except for murderers, the option to move into them or face jail time. Most Restricted Zones lack proper policing and regulation and are controlled by gangs dealing in Alternative Reality drugs and illegal cloning.

The lawlessness of Restricted Zones makes them popular with eJunkies who are desperate for new Black Market experiences. But, most Zones are too dangerous even for eJunkies to enter. Until recently, Restricted Zone 69 remained an exception. Controlled by one gang, the Constables, with Coco's brother Sam as its leader, the Zone remained peaceful enough for those seeking illegal adventure to risk arrest.

"Through sheer cunning, power, and might, Sammy's leadership brought order to Restricted Zone 69," says Coco.

Coco, one of the first generation of people to have been raised in Restricted Zone 69, worries for her life now that her brother is no longer in control. A recent assassination attempt on Sam has triggered a war between the Constables and rival gangs like the Matadors and the G-Raiders as each looks to expand its authority.

Coco knows Restricted Zone 69 well and can attest to the fluctuating levels of violence over the years. Her parents, Marcus and Tilda Trenchent, dealt in the illegal distribution of narcotics throughout the Free Zone and chose to live there rather than serve 20 years in prison. Over twenty years ago, they packed up their suburban townhouse and moved their two small children, Coco and Sam, to the gang-infested area to avoid incarceration.

Their parents, both skilled in healthcare, initially worked at the Restricted Zone Health Clinics that ran in donations from the World Corporation Organization (W.C.O.) According to Coco, "It didn't take too long before Dad was murdered by crooks trying to steal medical supplies. Without him working for the local health clinic, we were barely scraping by on meager stipends from the W.C.O., most of which was paid as protection money to the Matadors, the gang that controlled the area where we lived. Unable to make ends meet, Mom started selling herself to keep us fed, until one day Sam found her dead in a pool of her own blood, a bloody, rusty pipe beside her cold, naked corpse."

After their mother's death, Sam joined another gang, the Constables, and became a soldier to protect himself and his sister. He swiftly rose through the ranks of the gang after building a reputation as a viscous fighter, willing to do whatever it took to survive.

According to Coco, Sam became good friends with fellow gang member Marvin Rodan, known for his Machiavellian ideas on seizing control of the essentially lawless zone.

"Sam and Marvin were very close. About as close as two men can be, if you get what I mean," says Coco, hinting at Sam's intimate relationship with Marvin. "If Marvin was the brain, then Sammy was the brawn, so to speak. The two forged a powerful alliance and took control of one of the most powerful gangs in the territory, eventually defeating all the other gangs to achieve total control.

For a good many years, none of the other gangs in Restricted Zone 69 would do dealings without Constable approval and offering a cut of their earnings as tribute to Sam. This helped the gang maintain power, and allowed them to expand by bribing authorities to gain illegal access to the adjacent Free Zones. Over time, Sam became a compassionate leader and a hero to the residents of Restricted Zone 69, judiciously sharing his ill-gotten earnings to help feed, clothe, and provide medical care and education for most of the residents.

"Sammy wanted to form a government in the Zone that could function independently of the W.C.O. and other Zones. Marvin helped Sammy make it happen." says Coco. "Sammy knew if he didn't do something, no one would. The residents of Restricted Zone 69 would continue to suffer with little support from the other Zones."

Residents of Restricted Zones are contained by a cyberwall and given a meager stipend of bits for food, energy, and basic resources. Of course, some say that this subsistence-level support actually encourages further lawlessness as residents of the Restricted Zones feel compelled to supplement their state-provided assistance.

Today, the majority of Restricted Zones have been issued Emo-Regs by the W.C.O. in an effort to curtail violence and to keep residents content, with one exception: Restricted Zone 69. Before the recent assassination attempt on Sam Trenchent's life, residents under his leadership opted to boycott the distribution of Emo-Regs. But, the attack on the formidable leader of the Constables, leaving him comatose and paralyzed, has forced these same folks to reconsider the decision. As violence in those Restricted Zones that have adopted Emo-Regs dwindles, bloodshed within Restricted Zone 69 is at an all-time high.

"Sammy believes Emo-Regs would weaken the people's will to survive and allow the W.C.O. to take control of the territory," explained Coco. "But since Sammy lost control of the gang, it's hard to know what to do moving forward."

When asked who she thinks tried to have Sam killed, Coco admits, "I don't know. Most everyone here loves Sammy."

Coco asserts that since the attack on Sam, violence has escalated fast. She has had her life threatened on a number of occasions.

"Restricted Zone 69 is now even more dangerous than when we first moved here. And the W.C.O. ain't doing shit about it!" Says Coco.

The Fate of the Restricted Zone 69 residents is unclear as the gang war continues to devour its residents and ambitious upstart arrivals like the Guardians of Pain scavenge for what remains. At the time of writing, all Free Press requests for comment from the W.C.O. Have received no response.

3
DREAM CELEBRITY

CHAPTER 2
DREAM CELEBRITY
THE JUNGLE ROOM
WELCOME, MR. HOLMES. YOUR PARTY IS WAITING. RIGHT THIS WAY.

BA-THUMP
BA-THUMP
HECTOR!
I WAS SURPRISED BY YOUR CALL.
THANKS FOR MEETING ME.
EVERYONE'S WEARING ONE, EXCEPT US.
I PREFER TO KEEP MY FEELINGS TO MYSELF.

THEN YOU'LL NEVER BE A GREAT ACTOR.
I'M BACK WORKING AT PARADISE LOST STUDIOS.
WHAT'S THAT?
A VIRTUAL REALITY PRODUCTION STUDIO. ONE OF THE FEW LEFT THAT HASN'T REPLACED REAL ACTORS WITH MACHINE HOLOGRAMS.
AND YOU?
MIKE OFFERED ME A JOB WITH A.R.I.S.
THAT'S SURPRISING! THEY FIRED YOU!
YEAH, WELL...
...LIFE'S FULL OF SURPRISES.
SPEAKING OF, WHAT'S NEW?
YOU HAVE NO IDEA.
WHAT WOULD YOU BE INVESTIGATING?
ISN'T THAT DANGEROUS?
THE GUARDIANS OF PAIN.
I'VE GOT TO TRY TORCH AGAIN!

I WAS IN A 19TH CENTURY TRAIN WRECK!
ONLY, EVERYTHING LOOKED SO FAMILIAR.
ONE OF THE PASSENGERS LOOKED LIKE YOU!
IMPOSSIBLE! I'M NOT THAT OLD!
HEH!
THAT'S WHAT MADE IT SO STRANGE.
YOU'RE FRYING YOUR BRAIN!
NO WONDER YOU'RE SEEING THINGS.
STOP DOSING.
IT'S SUICIDE!

DON'T WORRY.
I'M NOT LIKE MY BROTHER.
SORRY.
WHAT'S REALLY BOTHERING YOU, HECTOR?
WE HAVEN'T SPOKEN IN YEARS.
NOW, OUT OF THE BLUE, YOU INVITE ME TO DINNER?
WERE YOU CHEATING ON MY BROTHER?
WHO TOLD YOU THAT?
NO...
...YOU DON'T.
LOOK, I DON'T CARE. I JUST WANT TO KNOW THE TRUTH.

IT WASN'T PERFECT, OUR RELATIONSHIP. IT WAS QUITE DIFFICULT, ACTUALLY.
YOU DON'T REMEMBER.
I DO.
IS THAT WHY HE TOOK HIS LIFE?
IF YOU'RE LOOKING TO BLAME SOMEONE...
...LOOK ELSEWHERE!
I'M DONE BEATING MYSELF UP OVER IT.
IF THERE'S SOMETHING YOU'RE NOT TELLING ME--
WHY DO YOU STILL WEAR THE RING?
GUILTY CONSCIENCE?
LET GO OF ME!
IT WAS A MISTAKE, SEEING YOU.

ALEX'S DEAD. MOVE ON!
IT'S TIME I DID TOO.



TINK
TNK
CLATTER



IT WAS YOUR MOTHER'S.

DREAM PALACE
WHERE'S GUMBY?
DON'T KNOW.
HE NEVER SHOWED UP FOR WORK.
NOBODY'S HEARD FROM HIM IN A FEW DAYS...
LOOK, HE OWES ME 1,000 BITS.
JUST TELL HIM HECTOR'S LOOKING FOR HIM, OK?
SALE
PARADISE
EVERY THING
THE TRUTH WILL SET YOU FREE
TRUTH WILL SET FREE
THE TRUTH WILL SET YOU FREE

SPLRT
SPLSH SPLSH
P.A.T.
PEOPLE AGAINST TECH
THE TRUTH WILL SET YOU FREE
PLSH
PLSH
PLSH
WILL SET YOU
FREE

YOU'VE GOT BALLS, SHOWING YOUR FACE AROUND HERE AFTER WHAT YOU DID TO SAM.
COME ON, MATRIX.
YOU DON'T THINK I WAS INVOLVED WITH THAT?
KRAK
VMMMMM

HELLO, HECTOR.
WHAT THE?
SHALE FRAK!
WHEN FACING DEATH, THEY SAY YOUR LIFE FLASHES BEFORE YOUR EYES.
NOT FOR AN eJUNKY.
FOR US, DEATH'S ANOTHER DÉJÀ VU.
THE END--? A NEW BEGINNING.
OUR EXPERIENCES INFLUENCE OUR MEMORIES AND DREAMS.
SHAPING OUR DECISIONS... OUR DESTINY...
...OUR QUESTIONS.
HOW DO YOU KNOW MY NAME?
VMMMMMMMMMMMMM

GO BACK
TO SLEEP,
HECTOR.

BEFORE
YOU GET
HURT.

CHHHHH

guuuhhh...

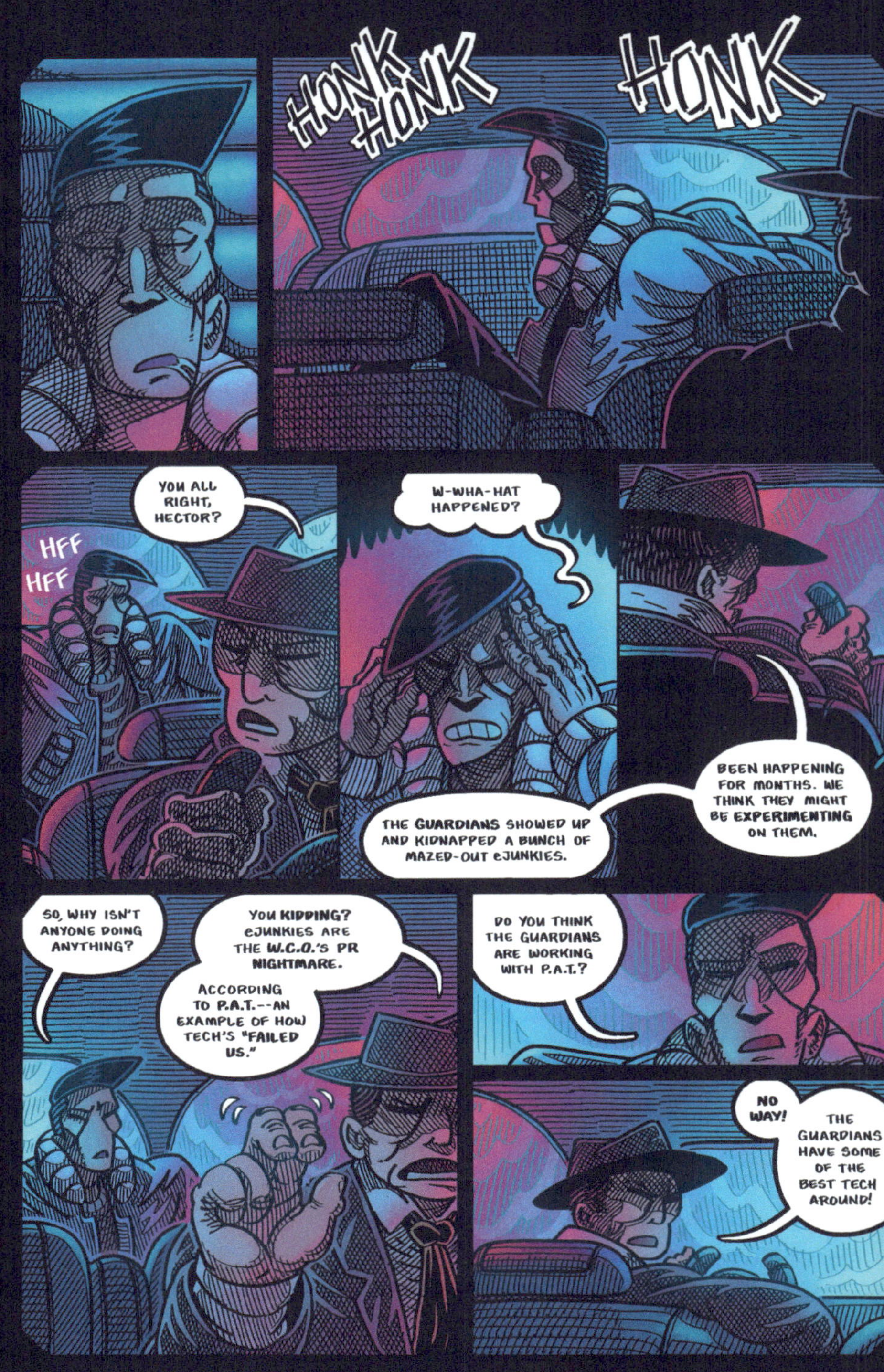

HONK
HONK
HONK
HONK


YOU ALL RIGHT, HECTOR?
HFF HFF
W-WHA-HAT HAPPENED?
BEEN HAPPENING FOR MONTHS. WE THINK THEY MIGHT BE EXPERIMENTING ON THEM.
THE GUARDIANS SHOWED UP AND KIDNAPPED A BUNCH OF MAZED-OUT eJUNKIES.
SO, WHY ISN'T ANYONE DOING ANYTHING?
YOU KIDDING? eJUNKIES ARE THE W.C.O.'S PR NIGHTMARE.
ACCORDING TO P.A.T.--AN EXAMPLE OF HOW TECH'S "FAILED US."
DO YOU THINK THE GUARDIANS ARE WORKING WITH P.A.T.?
NO WAY! THE GUARDIANS HAVE SOME OF THE BEST TECH AROUND!

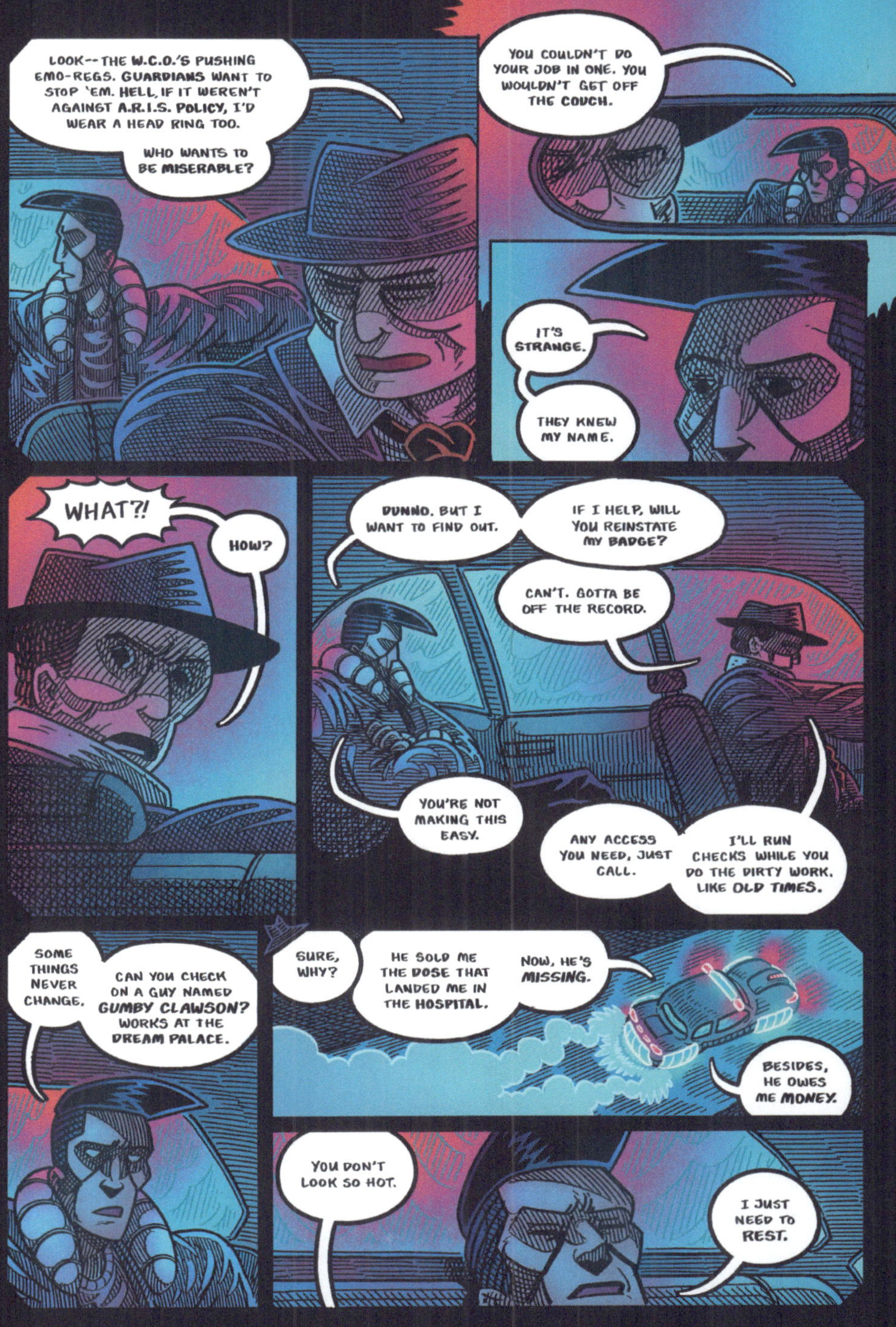

LOOK--THE W.C.O.'S PUSHING EMO-REGS. GUARDIANS WANT TO STOP 'EM. HELL, IF IT WEREN'T AGAINST A.R.I.S. POLICY, I'D WEAR A HEAD RING TOO.
WHO WANTS TO BE MISERABLE?
YOU COULDN'T DO YOUR JOB IN ONE. YOU WOULDN'T GET OFF THE COUCH.
IT'S STRANGE.
THEY KNEW MY NAME.
WHAT?!
HOW?
DUNNO. BUT I WANT TO FIND OUT.
IF I HELP, WILL YOU REINSTATE MY BADGE?
CAN'T. GOTTA BE OFF THE RECORD.
YOU'RE NOT MAKING THIS EASY.
ANY ACCESS YOU NEED, JUST CALL.
I'LL RUN CHECKS WHILE YOU DO THE DIRTY WORK. LIKE OLD TIMES.
SOME THINGS NEVER CHANGE.
CAN YOU CHECK ON A GUY NAMED GUMBY CLAWSON? WORKS AT THE DREAM PALACE.
SURE, WHY?
HE SOLD ME THE DOSE THAT LANDED ME IN THE HOSPITAL.
NOW, HE'S MISSING.
BESIDES, HE OWES ME MONEY.
YOU DON'T LOOK SO HOT.
I JUST NEED TO REST.

I WANT TO EXPRESS MY DEEP CONDOLENCES TO ANYONE WHO LOST SOMEONE DURING THE RECENT TRAGEDY.
ASTRA'S DREAMSCAPE CANCELLED
NEW EVIDENCE LINKS THE LATEST VICTIM OF TORCH...
HORK
...DOCTOR CASSANDRA MOORE, WITH THE GUARDIANS OF PAIN.
DOCTOR MOORE IS CURRENTLY BEING TREATED...
THE DOCTOR MAY HAVE BEEN STEALING CHEMICALS FROM HER HOSPITAL'S LABORATORY, WHICH THE GUARDIANS USED TO MAKE TORCH.
...AT THE L.A. CENTER FOR BEHAVIORAL AND PSYCHIATRIC STUDIES..
DR. CASSANDRA MOORE
...WHERE SHE REMAINS IN A COMA AFTER TAKING AN ILLEGAL DOSE.
WHAT THE HELL?

CENTER FOR BEHAVIORAL
AND PSYCHIATRIC STUDIES
LOS ANGELES, CALIFORNIA.
EMERGENCY SERVICES
NEGATIVE.
YOU ARE ALREADY IN THE SYSTEM AS AN APPROVED VISITOR.
YOU ALREADY HAVE CLEARANCE, MR. HOLMES.
MY BADGE'S BEEN REINSTATED?
THIS KEEPS GETTING WEIRDER.

WHY ARE YOU REALLY HERE, HECTOR?
TWO YEARS EARLIER...
I TOLD YOU.
I HAVE A PROBLEM.

YOU TOLD ME THAT YOU GOT FIRED BECAUSE YOU WERE ADDICTED TO ALTERNATIVE CELLMEM EXPERIENCES...
...AND THAT LED YOU TO START STEALING THEM WHILE ON DUTY.
BUT...
...YOU NEVER TOLD ME YOU HAD A PROBLEM.
WHAT DO YOU MEAN?
I THINK A DEEPER PART OF YOU ALREADY KNOWS THE TRUTH.
THE TRUTH?
THAT SOMETIMES, TO EMBRACE YOUR PAIN-- TO FACE IT--IS THE ONLY WAY TO HEAL.
THE ONLY WAY TO GROW.
YOUR PROBLEM ISN'T THAT YOU'RE SEEKING OUT REAL EMOTIONAL EXPERIENCES, PAINFUL ONES EVEN.
YOUR PROBLEM IS THAT YOU'RE BRAINWASHED INTO THINKING THAT IT'S WRONG.
YOU'RE DROWNING OUT THE DEEPER PART OF YOURSELF.
BUT, THERE'S HOPE.

"I'D LIKE TO INTRODUCE YOU TO SOMEONE I THINK CAN HELP."
YOU DON'T LOOK SO GOOD, DOC.
LET'S SEE WHAT HAPPENED TO YOU...
...MAYBE FIND A CLUE AS TO HOW YOU ENDED UP HERE.

WHO...
...IS THAT?
GUESS I'M BEING WATCHED.
BETTER GO WHERE I WON'T BE DISTURBED.

INITIALIZING...
EVERY DOSE IS DANGEROUS.
THIS ONE PUT DOCTOR MOORE IN A COMA, SO IT MUST BE PRETTY PAINFUL.
GOOD THING I LIKE IT THAT WAY.

TINK
TINK

APRIL 15, 1912, 2:20 AM. 370 MILES SOUTH-SOUTHEAST OF NEWFOUNDLAND, NORTH ATLANTIC OCEAN.
R.M.S. TITANIC
R.M.S. TITANIC
WHERE AM I?

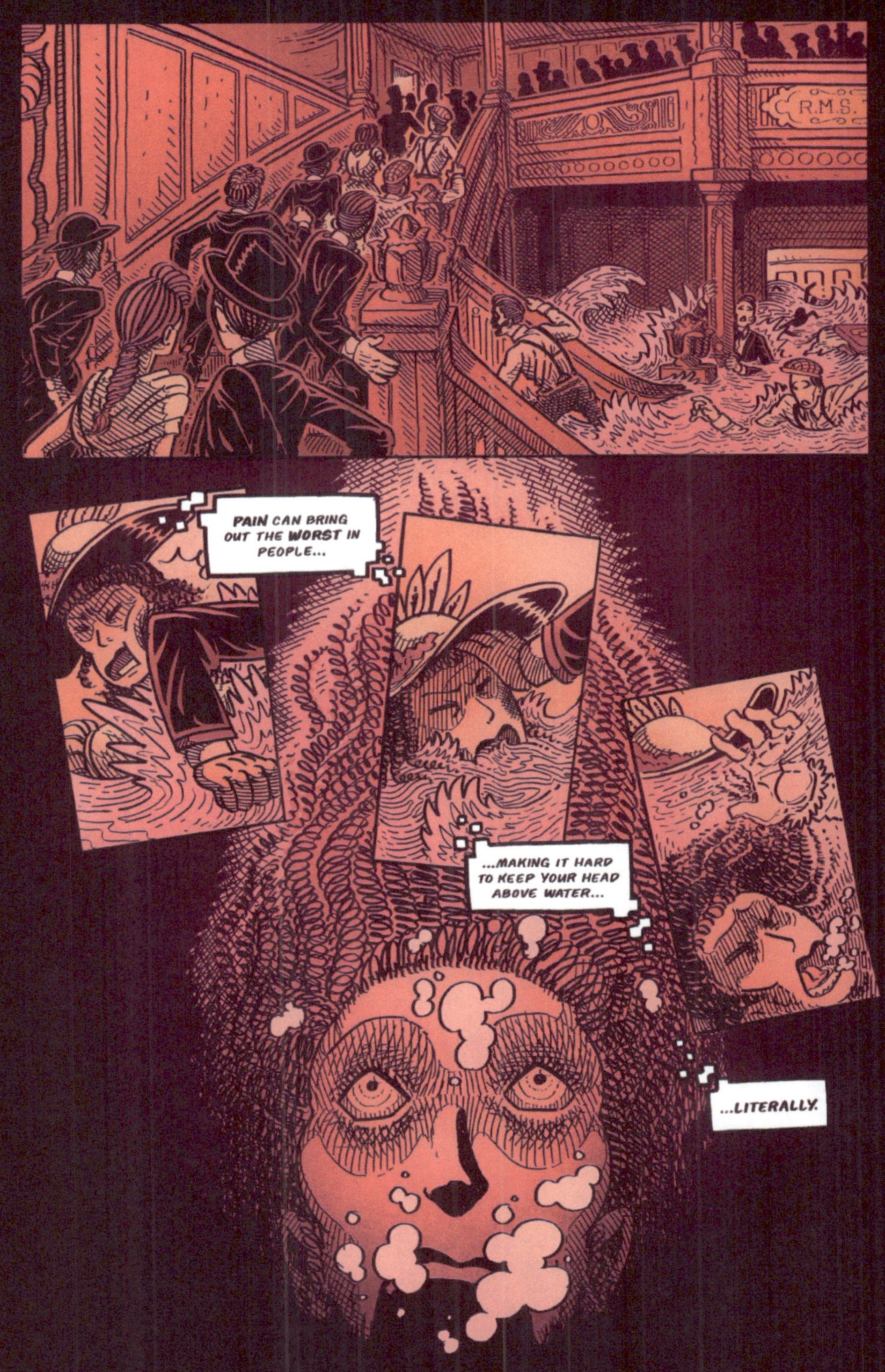

R.M.S.
PAIN CAN BRING OUT THE WORST IN PEOPLE...
...MAKING IT HARD TO KEEP YOUR HEAD ABOVE WATER...
...LITERALLY.

GRRR
HVFF
HVFF HVFF
CLIK
CLIK
CLIK
THAT EXPERIENCE FELT WAY TOO SHORT.
SOMETHING'S NOT RIGHT.
WHATEVER HAPPENED, SHE WASN'T ALONE.
SOMEONE'S TAMPERED WITH HER EXPERIENCE.
TERROR HAS STRUCK AGAIN...
BREAKING NEWS!
...FORCING THE CELEBRITY TO CANCEL HER POPULAR DREAM SHOW UNTIL FURTHER NOTICE.
...AS THE GUARDIANS OF PAIN CONTINUE TO HACK INTO ASTRA'S DREAM CHANNEL...
ASTRA ISSUES OFFIC APOLOGY TO HER FA

*RING RING*
HELLO, MIKE MILLER.
TRACKED DOWN YOUR BOY GUMBY.
WHAT?!
FOUND HIM LYING IN A DITCH, UNDER JUNKY BRIDGE.
A LETHAL DOSE OF BOTH TORCH AND EXTRANOL IN HIS BODY.
TELL HIM I'M GONNA KILL HIM.
TOO LATE. HE'S ALREADY DEAD.
WHAT ABOUT DOCTOR MOORE?

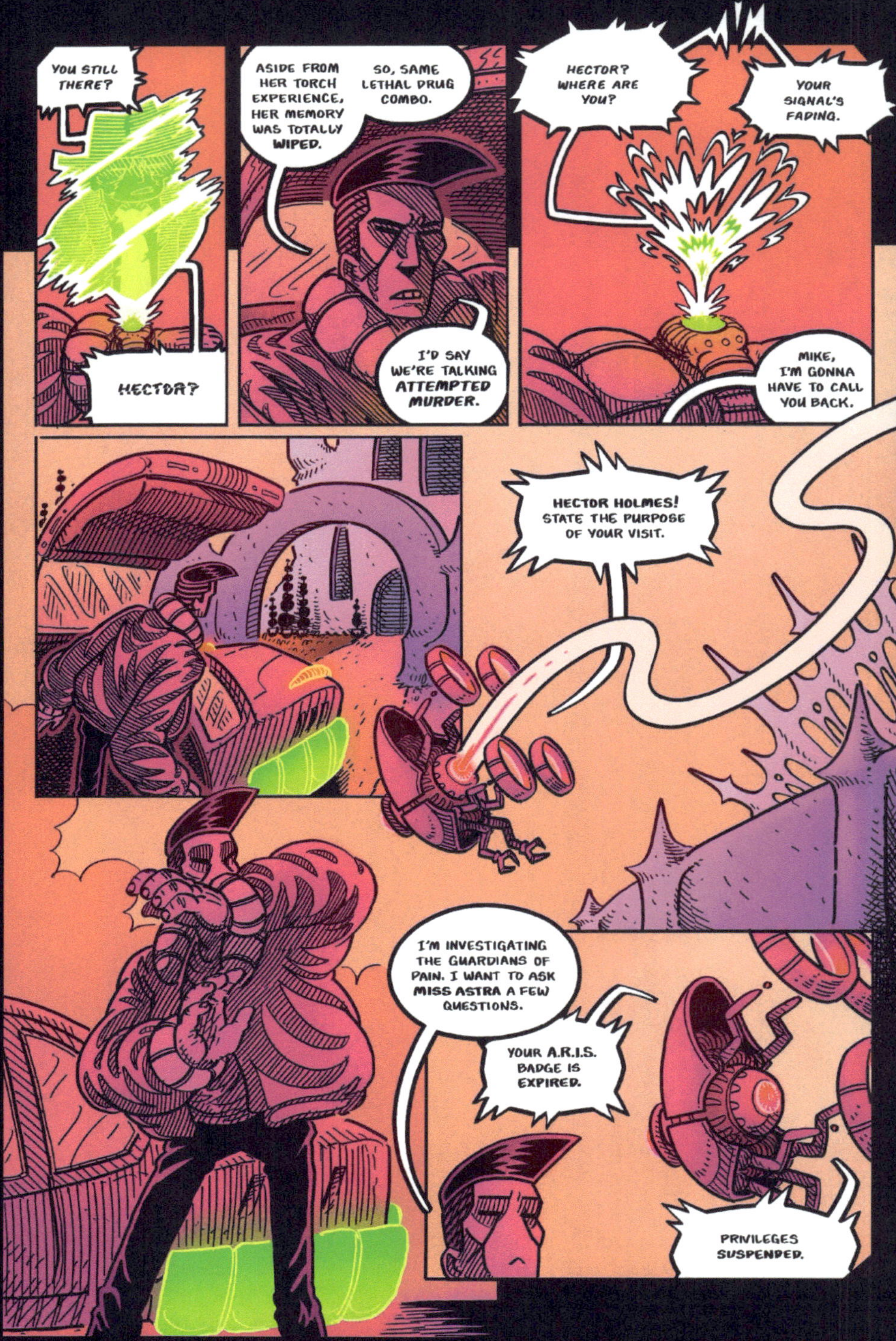

YOU STILL THERE?
HECTOR?
ASIDE FROM HER TORCH EXPERIENCE, HER MEMORY WAS TOTALLY WIPED.
SO, SAME LETHAL DRUG COMBO.
I'D SAY WE'RE TALKING ATTEMPTED MURDER.
HECTOR? WHERE ARE YOU?
YOUR SIGNAL'S FADING.
MIKE, I'M GONNA HAVE TO CALL YOU BACK.
HECTOR HOLMES! STATE THE PURPOSE OF YOUR VISIT.
I'M INVESTIGATING THE GUARDIANS OF PAIN. I WANT TO ASK MISS ASTRA A FEW QUESTIONS.
YOUR A.R.I.S. BADGE IS EXPIRED.
PRIVILEGES SUSPENDED.

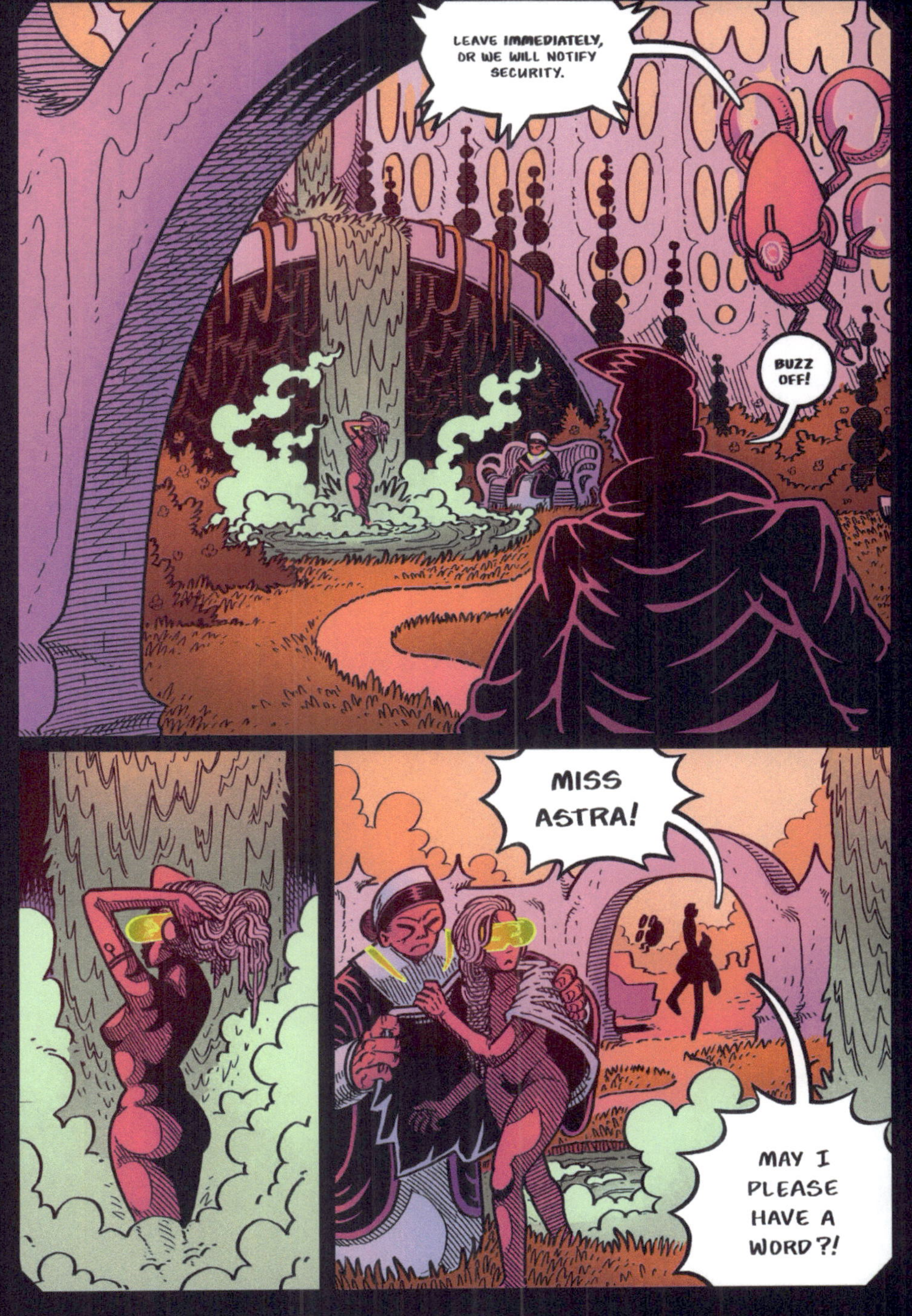

LEAVE IMMEDIATELY, OR WE WILL NOTIFY SECURITY.
BUZZ OFF!
MISS ASTRA!
MAY I PLEASE HAVE A WORD?!

MY NAME IS HECTOR HOLMES.
I'M ONLY HERE TO HELP.
OH!
TUMULT!
YOU, SIR, LEAVE AT ONCE!
THIS IS PRIVATE PROPERTY!
I'VE SEEN THEM.

THESE GUARDIANS.
OH!
GHRK!
WAIT!
YOU'VE SEEN THEM, TOO?

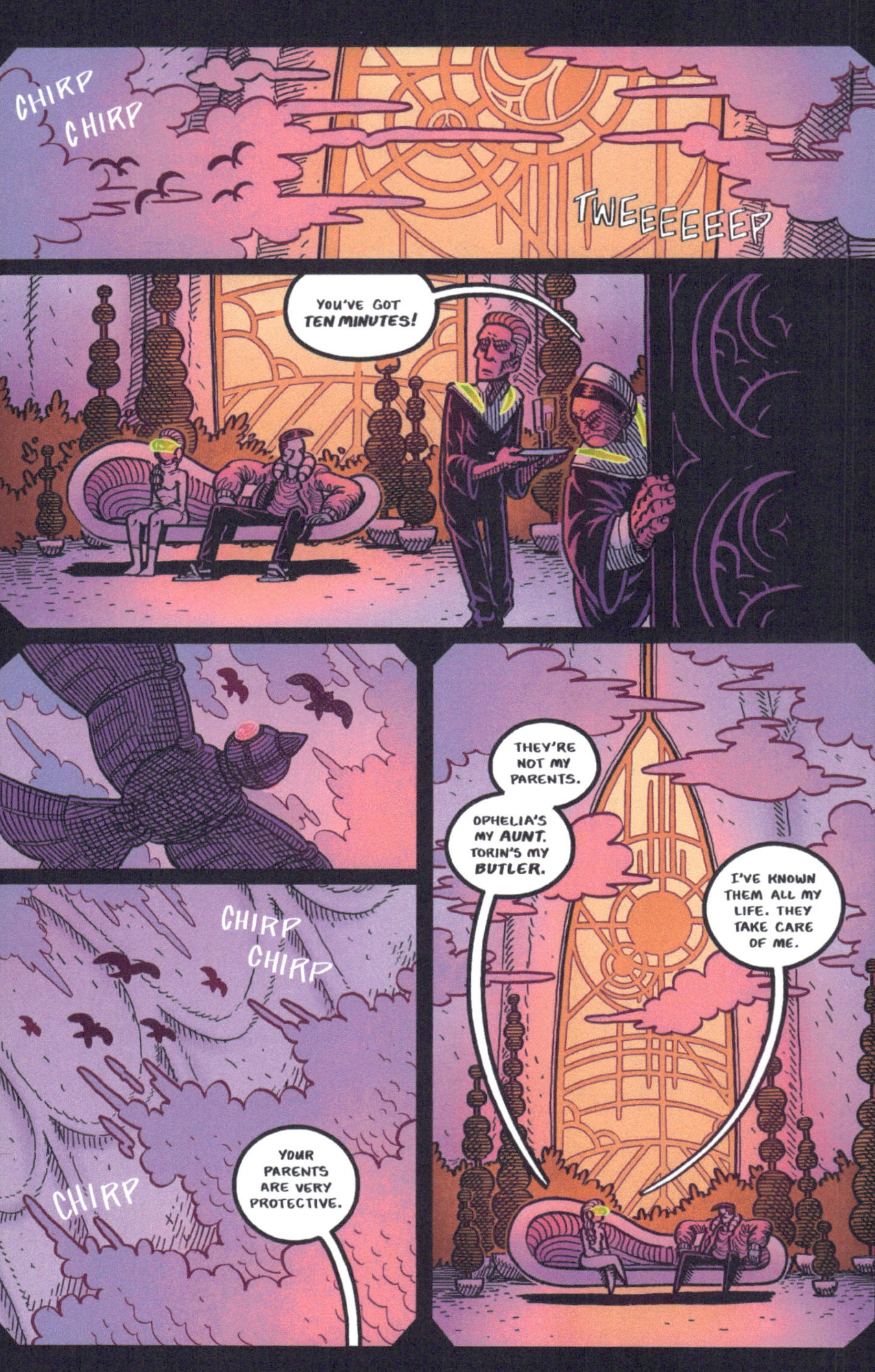

CHIRP
CHIRP
TWEEEEEEP
YOU'VE GOT
TEN MINUTES!
CHIRP
CHIRP
CHIRP
YOUR
PARENTS
ARE VERY
PROTECTIVE.
THEY'RE
NOT MY
PARENTS.
OPHELIA'S
MY AUNT.
TORIN'S MY
BUTLER.
I'VE KNOWN
THEM ALL MY
LIFE. THEY
TAKE CARE
OF ME.

WHAT ABOUT YOUR PARENTS?
THEY DIED WHEN I WAS LITTLE.
CAR CRASH.
I'M SORRY.
THAT'S WHAT YOU'RE SUPPOSED TO SAY, RIGHT?
WHY ARE YOU LOOKING AT ME THAT WAY?
I'VE NEVER MET AN INNOCENT BEFORE.
I'M ONE OF THE FIRST, YOU KNOW.
PLACED IN AN EMO-REG THE MINUTE I WAS BORN.
THEY SAY I NEVER CRIED.
I BET YOU WERE NEVER SPANKED EITHER.
SPANKED?
I MEANT, YOU'VE CLEARLY LIVED A CHARMED LIFE.
YOU'RE RIGHT.

UNTIL RECENTLY, MY EXPERIENCES WERE NOTHING BUT GOOD DREAMS.
NO PAIN...
...LOSS...
...OR FEAR.
ONLY PEACE AND LOVE.
I WOULDN'T KNOW WHAT THAT'S LIKE.
I'M WHAT PEOPLE CALL AN eJUNKY.
ALWAYS CHASING THE NEXT EXPERIENCE.
IS THAT WHY YOU BECAME AN A.R.I.S.?
PARTLY. ALSO FOLLOWING IN MY BROTHER'S FOOTSTEPS.
YOUR BROTHER'S AN A.R.I.S. TOO?
WAS.
HE DIED.

OH.
I'VE NEVER KNOWN ANYONE WHO DIED.
EVERYONE DIES.
CHIRP
CHIRP
CHEEEEP
FLASH

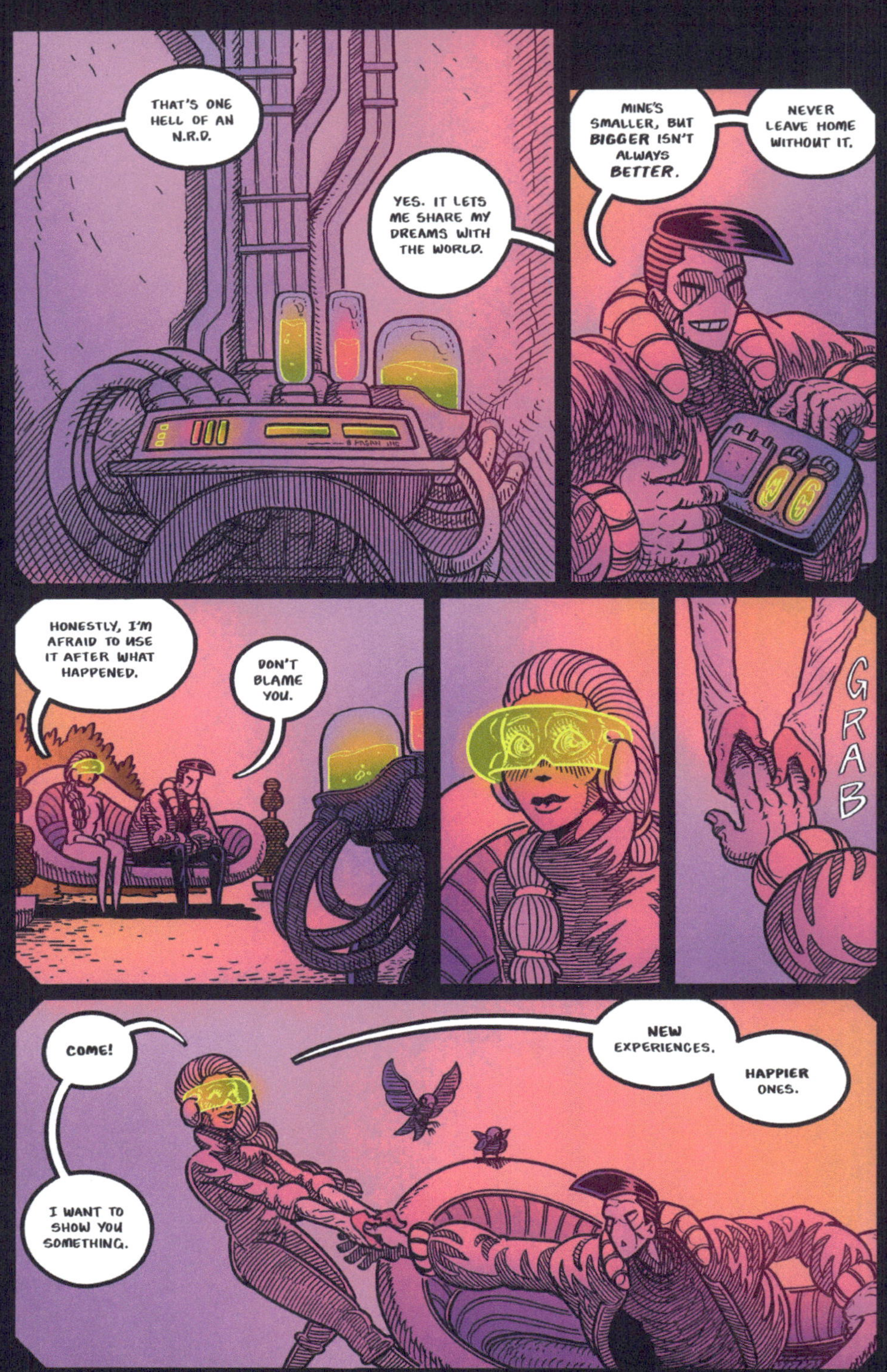

THAT'S ONE HELL OF AN N.R.D.
YES. IT LETS ME SHARE MY DREAMS WITH THE WORLD.
MINE'S SMALLER, BUT BIGGER ISN'T ALWAYS BETTER.
NEVER LEAVE HOME WITHOUT IT.
HONESTLY, I'M AFRAID TO USE IT AFTER WHAT HAPPENED.
DON'T BLAME YOU.
GRAB
COME!
I WANT TO SHOW YOU SOMETHING.
NEW EXPERIENCES.
HAPPIER ONES.

WELCOME TO
MY WORLD!
WOW!
AN ENTIRE
PALACE BUILT
ON DREAMS.

WITH THIS, YOU CAN FLOAT ANYWHERE!
BEEP
TRY IT!
BEEP
THE W.C.O. HASN'T ALLOWED PUBLIC DISTRIBUTION YET, BUT I GOT ONE.
THEY SEND ME LOTS OF THINGS!
HOPING YOU'LL DREAM ABOUT IT, I'M SURE.
GOOD PUBLICITY!
HA HA
HA
HA HA
HA!
HA!
LOOK!

fwap
fwap
BUMP
HA HA HA!
HA HA HA HA!
PUSH
WHAT'S WRONG? AREN'T YOU HAVING FUN?
HOW DO I GET DOWN?

PRESS THE BUTTON!
HEH, HEH. YOU SHOULD REALLY WAIT UNTIL YOU'RE CLOSER TO THE FLOOR!
ARE YOU UPSET?
NO...
...BUT, I DIDN'T COME HERE TO PLAY.
CRASH
I'M HERE ABOUT THE GUARDIANS.
WHY DO THEY WANT TO HURT ME?
THEY'RE REVOLUTIONARIES.
MY AUNT CALLS THEM TERRORISTS.
I SUPPOSE THAT DEPENDS ON YOUR PERSPECTIVE.
WHAT DO THEY WANT?
TO STOP PEOPLE FROM WEARING EMO-REGS.
WHY?

EMO-REGS MAKE PEOPLE APATHETIC. THOSE PEOPLE WHO DIED WATCHING YOUR SHOW DIDN'T EVEN TRY TO ESCAPE.
WHO'S ABLE TO GET CLOSE TO YOU-- BESIDES YOUR BUTLER AND AUNT?
TUMULT, MY DRIVER.
WHERE'S HE DRIVE YOU?
AT LEAST THEY WEREN'T SCARED.
COME TO THINK OF IT... NOWHERE, REALLY.
YOU SURE HE'S NOT YOUR BODYGUARD?
WHY WOULD I NEED A BODYGUARD?
THERE ARE A LOT OF BAD PEOPLE OUT THERE.
ARE YOU A BAD PERSON?

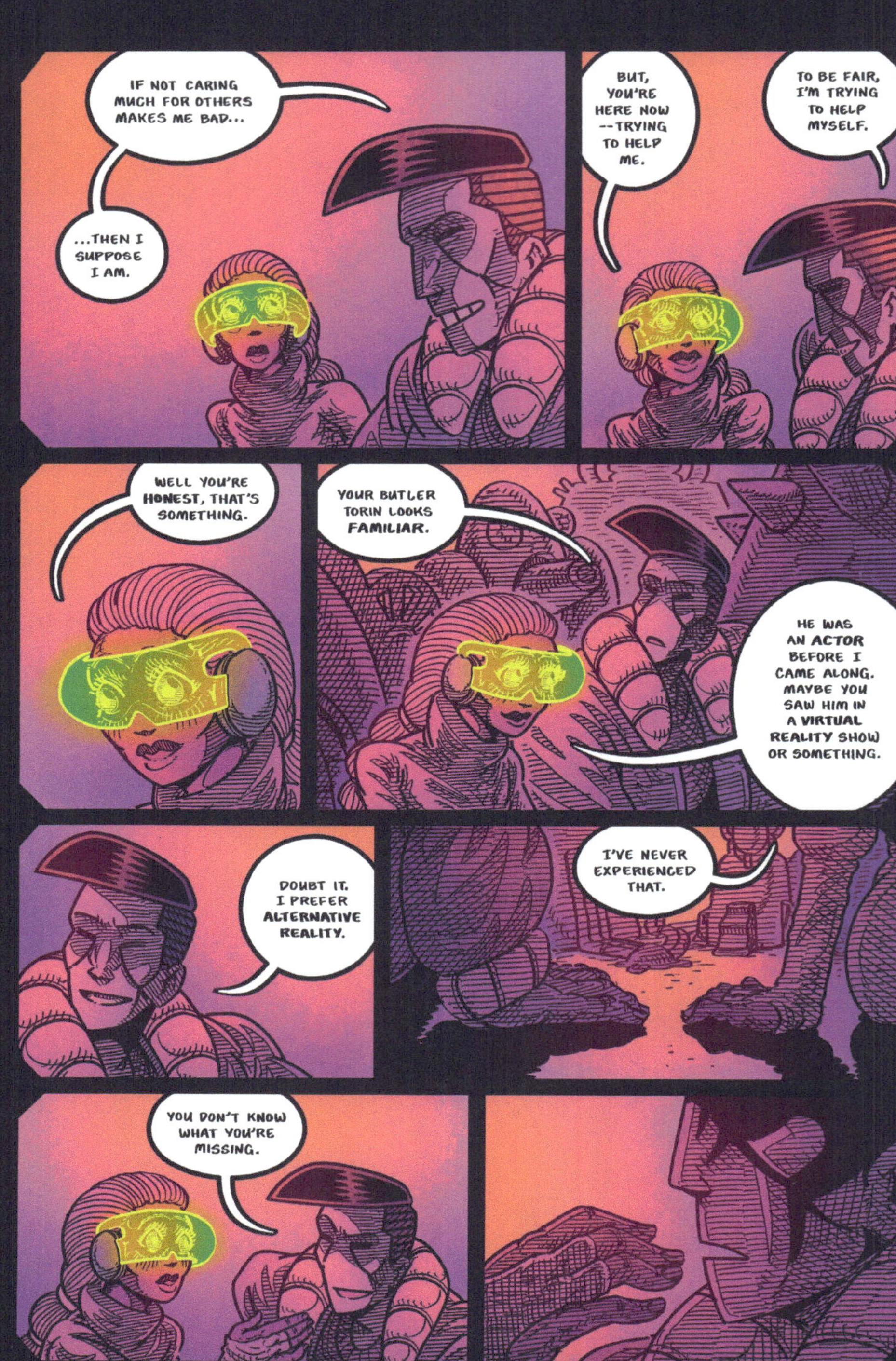

IF NOT CARING MUCH FOR OTHERS MAKES ME BAD...
...THEN I SUPPOSE I AM.
BUT, YOU'RE HERE NOW --TRYING TO HELP ME.
TO BE FAIR, I'M TRYING TO HELP MYSELF.
WELL YOU'RE HONEST, THAT'S SOMETHING.
YOUR BUTLER TORIN LOOKS FAMILIAR.
HE WAS AN ACTOR BEFORE I CAME ALONG. MAYBE YOU SAW HIM IN A VIRTUAL REALITY SHOW OR SOMETHING.
DOUBT IT. I PREFER ALTERNATIVE REALITY.
I'VE NEVER EXPERIENCED THAT.
YOU DON'T KNOW WHAT YOU'RE MISSING.

ENOUGH OF THESE GAMES!
WE WERE JUST GETTING STARTED.
NONSENSE! I SEE WHERE THIS IS LEADING, AND I DON'T LIKE IT!
TUMULT! SEE THIS MAN TO THE GATE!
LOOK, ASTRA, TAKE MY INFO.
I THINK WE CAN HELP EACH OTHER.

DO YOU CARE ABOUT HER?
HER AUNT MAY HAVE GOOD INTENTIONS, BUT SHE DOESN'T UNDERSTAND THE THREAT HERE.
I CAN HELP.
SHOVE
THAT WENT WELL.

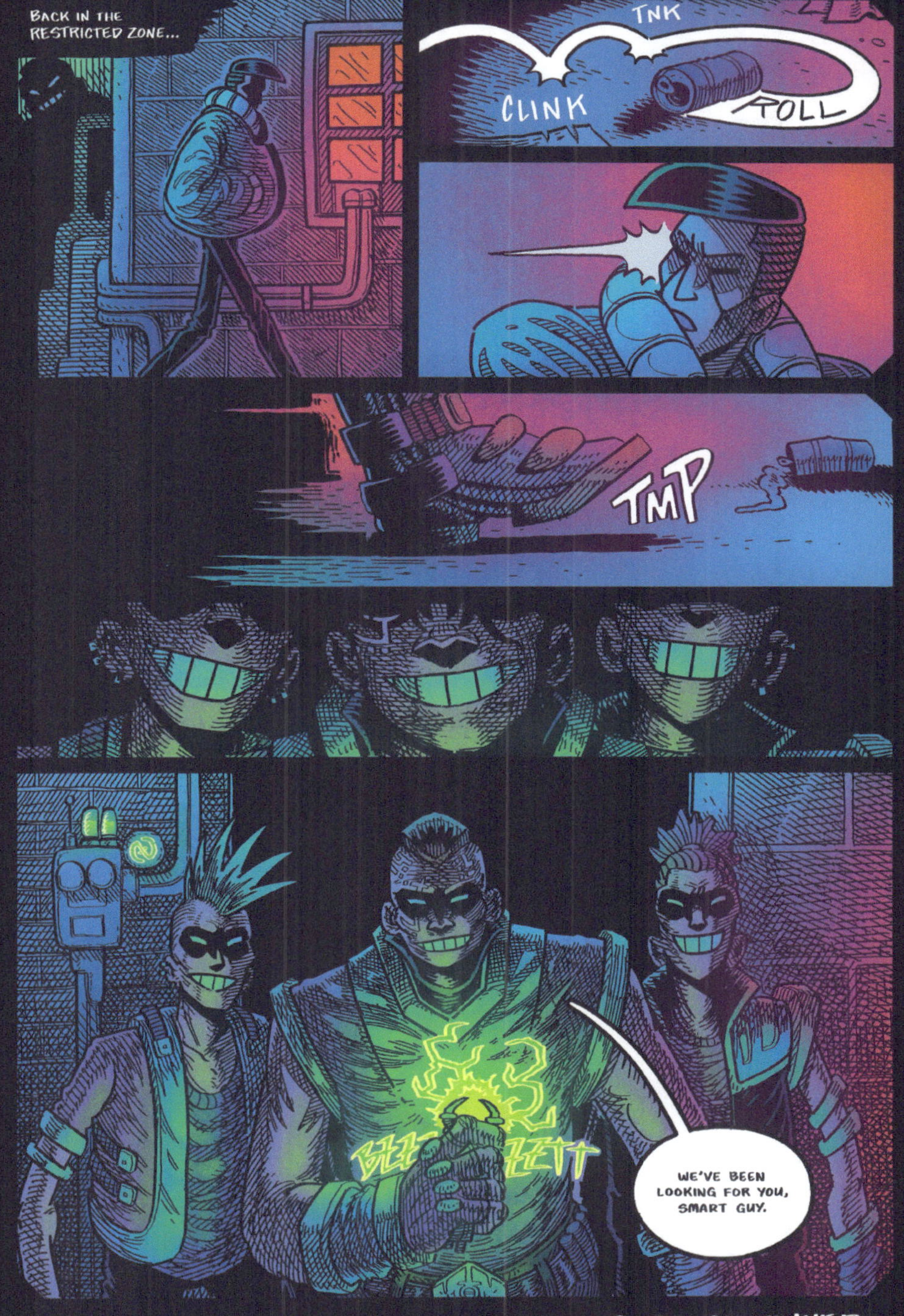

BACK IN THE RESTRICTED ZONE...
TNK
CLINK
ROLL
TMP
WE'VE BEEN LOOKING FOR YOU, SMART GUY.
BZZ—ZZTT
TO BE CONTINUED...
077

EMORFG

EMO R

WITH INS 2.0

PEACE OF MIND COMES FROM KNOWING YOU'RE IN CONTROL OF HOW YOU FEEL!

EMOTIONAL REGULATION IS PROVEN TO PROVIDE LONGER-LASTING PEACE AND HAPPINESS! WHILE OTHER BRANDS ARE ONLY NOW ENTERING THE MARKET, OUR EMO-REGS ARE TRIED AND TESTED AND WILL PERMIT YOU TO FEEL A WHOLE RANGE OF EMOTIONS--WITHOUT THE PAINFUL, HARMFUL SIDE EFFECTS OF ANXIETY, DEPRESSION, AND FEAR!

ERADICATE MOODINESS AND ANXIETY WITH PAGAN INC.'S PATENTED DESIGNS. AUGMENT YOUR MEMORIES AND EXPERIENCES WHILE THEY HAPPEN TO YOU! DESIGNED TO ENHANCE DESIRE, NOT ELIMINATE IT, BY ERASING EMOTIONAL RISKS.

OUR REALITY-BLOCKING VISORS USE SUBCUTANEOUSLY CONNECTED FEEDBACK SENSORS TO TRACK YOUR EMOTIONAL REACTIONS TO PAINFUL IMAGES AND WORK TO ERASE THEM SO YOU NEVER HAVE TO SEE THEM AGAIN.

PATENTED GALVANIC SKIN RESPONSE (GSR) INSIDE THE HALO BAND DETECTS CHANGES IN SWEAT GLAND ACTIVITY, ASSIGNING COLORS TO EACH EMOTION.

FEATURES INSEAM SENSORS (INS 2.0) TO BE SURE EVERYONE INSTANTLY KNOWS HOW YOU FEEL TO AVOID CONFRONTATION AND CONFUSION.

NEVER BE AFRAID TO SHOW YOUR AUTHENTIC SELF! WHAT DO YOU HAVE TO HIDE?

The Guardians are radical critics of the W.C.O. and its proposed mandate that would require everyone to wear EMO-REGs. They made a point to use the recent tragedy as an example of the deadly risks posed to humanity as a result of forcing people to wear EMO-REGs. The Guardians are not alone in their protest. Other zones have voted against the mandate requiring EMO-REGs to be worn. These include Zone 1, known also as "The Free Zone," where most of the residents typically vote against mandates requiring the use of technology. The Free Zone is where the leaders of The People Against Technology reside and is also where the group has staged most of its protests.

Leaders of The Free Zone caution against the mandate noting, "Wherever EMO-REGs have been adopted, there are higher unemployment rates, as people lack the motivation to work. Spending on other forms of entertainment and social interaction, even eating, has diminished."

Recognizing that these are real issues for society, Pagan Inc., inventors of the EMO-REG, has reportedly "worked hard to dial back the effectiveness of the emotional regulation in their devices" in recent months. The company agrees that a certain level of desire and discomfort may be necessary to keep people motivated to live healthy and productive lives. Spokespersons for Pagan Inc., including Gideon Mars, the company's CEO, are quick to point out the effectiveness of EMO-REGs in reducing crime, domestic abuse, and suicide.

For their part, P.A.T. has long argued that EMO-REGs are dangerous. They deny any association with The Guardians of Pain "who violate P.A.T.'s core beliefs" as outlined in their manifesto, which "strictly forbids any use of alternative reality drugs" like Torch. Surprisingly, many companies within the W.C.O. itself have financed P.A.T.'s efforts to fight the W.C.O.'s emotional regulation mandate. Their ranks include companies like Yummytime Inc., a food company behind the Yo Yo Rama Ring Dings popular with kids. After a reduced earnings report, citing a drop in sales due to children wearing EMO-REGs making them "uninterested" in their products, the company's stock plunged. As a result, Yummytime Inc. has reportedly laid off 48% of its workforce. One employee was happy to comment, "I didn't mind, really." This rather blasé response didn't come as much of a surprise when he later told me that the company issued him a free EMO-REG to ease his burden. When I asked him what he hopes to do next, he shrugged.

Now personally, I love my EMO-REG. It makes me feel, well, good. However, there are occasions when I choose not to wear it. Let's take today, for example. If I were to have worn my EMO-REG today, I would likely be far too complacent to write this article. I know you're supposed to be able to dial back the mood-enhancing stabilizers and adjust the normalization levels, but I haven't figured out how to balance being happy and fulfilled without ruining my desire to do my job. Judging by conversations with colleagues and friends, I'm not alone.



In an interview with Astra after the hack, the dream celebrity admitted, "I feel used and sad. My only solace is knowing that thanks to EMO-REGs, nobody suffered. I'm worried they'll try it again. Now, I have nightmares and the producers have canceled my show." Other producers are doing the same. Jupiter Sound, Mood Metal, Neon Light, and Godbrain have all canceled their dream projections as well. Security has been tightened on the few who remain in business.

The impact of Astra's dream hack has created a ripple within the dream celebrity community. Dream celebrities are popular because their dreams are pure pleasure. Many dream celebrities are given EMO-REGs at a young age to keep their dreams that way. The recent hack changed that, causing significant concerns among some producers and dream celebrities. If dream celebrities are riddled with nightmares, this spells trouble for fans looking to them for escape. Still, if the recent mandate requiring EMO-REGs passes, it's possible these fears will quickly fade.

Then again, so may our desire for dream celebrities altogether.

# 3

## THE NIGHTMARE

CHAPTER 3
THE NIGHTMARE
SNIFF
SNIFF

SNATCH

WE'VE BEEN LOOKING FOR YOU.
BUZZ
ZZZT

YOU CRAWLED OUT OF THE RESTRICTED ZONE LOOKING FOR ME?
I'M SHOCKED, REALLY.
NO, YOU'RE NOT--
--BUT YOU ARE NOW!
CRACKLE
UUUUGHH...

GH—
NGH
CLICK
THOKK
I SAW YOU WITH THOSE GUARDIANS.
THEY KNEW YOUR NAME.
CLIK
VERY STRANGE THE WAY YOU RAN OUT AFTER SAMMY WAS SHOT.
I-I HAD N-NOTHING TO DO WITH IT!
YEEE-AAAHH!!

ZAK
SHAZBOT!
HRRK

BRRR
GNH!
GNH!
THVMP

NOW IT'S MY TURN TO ASK QUESTIONS!
MARVIN'S THE BOSS NOW THAT SAMMY'S OUT OF THE PICTURE, RIGHT?
CHK
ZAP
YOU'RE--
--UUGH--
--MAKING A BIG MISTAKE.
I'VE MADE A LOT OF MISTAKES.
BUT TAZING YOUR FUTURE GENERATIONS OUT OF EXISTENCE WON'T BE ONE OF THEM.

WHAT THE--
DON'T JUST STAND THERE!
GET HIM!
WHOA, EASY THERE. LET'S TA--
WHOA, EASY THERE. LET'S TA--

WHAM
STOP!
YOU DON'T KNOW WHO YOU'RE MESSING WITH!

UUGH...


WHY DID
YOU FOLLOW
ME?

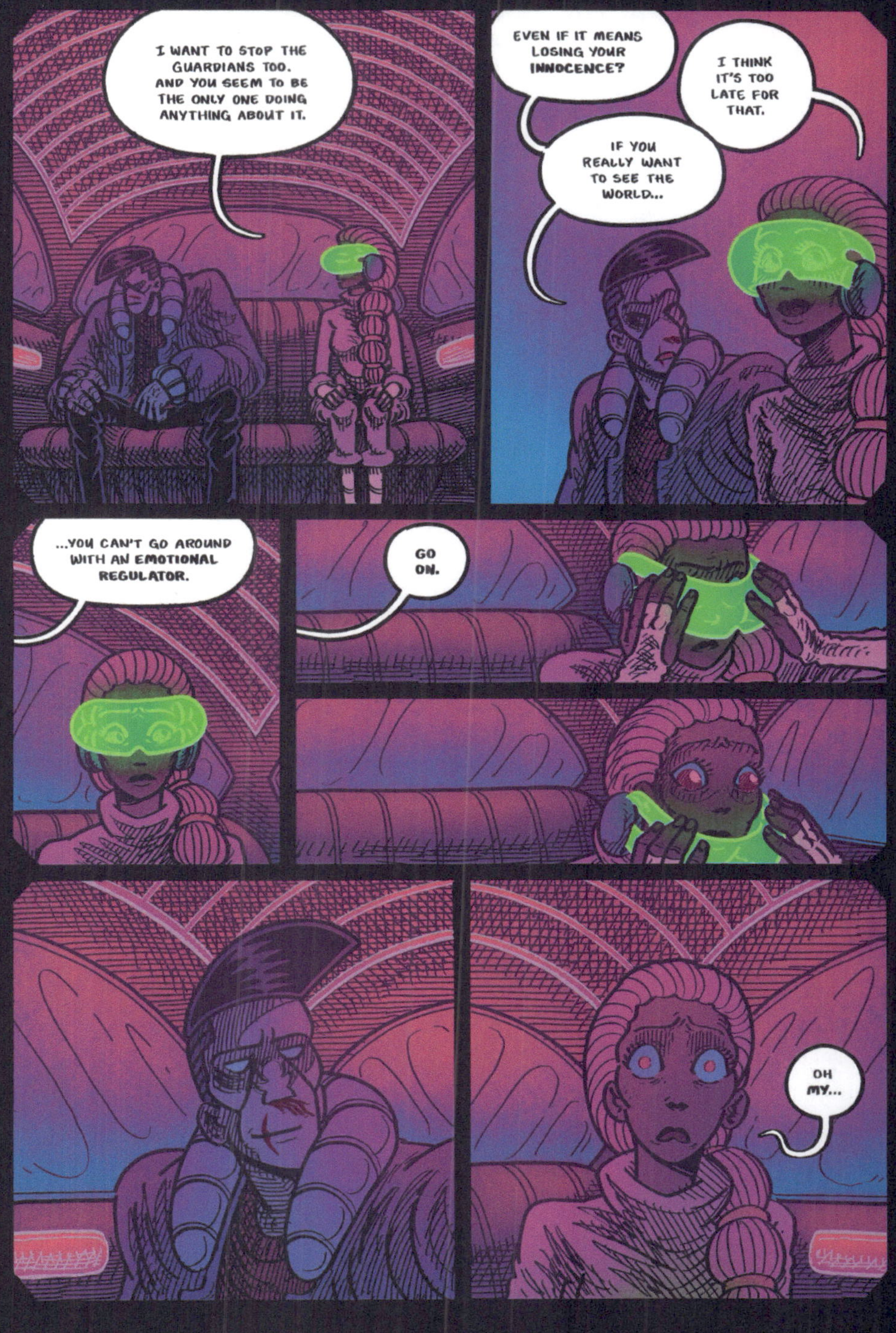

I WANT TO STOP THE GUARDIANS TOO. AND YOU SEEM TO BE THE ONLY ONE DOING ANYTHING ABOUT IT.
EVEN IF IT MEANS LOSING YOUR INNOCENCE?
I THINK IT'S TOO LATE FOR THAT.
IF YOU REALLY WANT TO SEE THE WORLD...
...YOU CAN'T GO AROUND WITH AN EMOTIONAL REGULATOR.
GO ON.
OH MY...

THAT'S HORRIBLE.
THAT'S LIFE.
THEY DIDN'T WANT ME TO FOLLOW YOU. BUT I DID ANYWAY.
AND TUMULT?
TUMULT DOES WHAT I SAY.
HE'S A CLONE.

HOW COULD YOU TELL?
HIS SKIN.
SURPRISED YOUR AUNT WAS OK WITH THAT. SHE'S PRETTY PROTECTIVE.
ACTUALLY, IT WAS HER DECISION FOR ME TO HAVE A CLONE.
WE'RE HIS FAMILY. PEOPLE DO ANYTHING FOR FAMILY.
HE'S HARMLESS.
MAYBE, TO YOU.
WHAT ARE YOU GOING TO DO NOW?
HEAD INTO THE RESTRICTED ZONE.
THERE'S SOMEONE I WANT TO SEE WHO MAY BE ABLE TO HELP US LEARN MORE ABOUT THESE GUARDIANS.

WE'LL GO
WITH YOU.

IT'S NOT
SAFE.

I CAN'T BE
SHELTERED
FOREVER.

BESIDES, WE
HAVE TUMULT!

IN THE RESTRICTED ZONE.

WHAT ARE
THOSE?

THAT'S WHERE
THEY LIVE.

MOST OF THEM
ARE ON W.G.O.
STIPENDS.

SPONSORSHIP FOR ADS IN
THE RESTRICTED ZONE
DOESN'T PAY WELL.

WHY AREN'T
THEY WEARING
EMO-REGS?

I THOUGHT THE
GOVERNMENT ISSUES
THEM TO ANYONE WHO
CAN'T AFFORD ONE?

HECTOR

TWO YEARS AGO...

HEY, SAM.

MATRIX.

WHERE'S THE UNIFORM?

GOT FIRED.

DON'T WORRY, SAM.

THEY KNOW NOTHING ABOUT US.

PROBABLY FOR THE BEST. A.R.I.S. IS SHIT, ANYWAY.

W.C.O. OWNS 'EM.

PRETENDING TO PROTECT US WITH THIS CENSOR 'BAD' EXPERIENCE BULLSHIT.

SO, WHATCHA GONNA DO NOW?

DON'T KNOW.

ANY CHANCE YOU CAN STILL HOOK ME UP?

YOU THINK I'M RUNNING A FREE SHOW?

YOU CAN'T OFFER ME PROTECTION ANYMORE.

KIDDING, FOOL!

I'LL STILL TAKE CARE OF YA.

HECTOR?
SORRY.
WHY AREN'T THEY WEARING EMO-REGS?
SOME FOLKS PREFER TO SEE THE WORLD THE WAY IT REALLY IS.
PEOPLE AGAINST TECHNOLO...
THE TRUTH WILL SET YOU FREE
THE TRUTH WILL SET YOU FREE...
WE'RE HERE.

DO YOU KNOW WHO YOU WERE CLONED FROM?
WHAT?
YOUR FAMILY.
DO YOU KNOW YOUR FAMILY?
SHE'S MY FAMILY.
SAFER TO PARK IT OUTSIDE THE DISTRICT.
IT'LL RETURN WHEN I SIGNAL IT.
LAUNDROMAT
KNOCK KNOCK
CREEEAK

YOU GOT A LOT OF NERVE SHOWING UP HERE.
MARVIN'LL HAVE YOUR HIDE!
HE THINKS YOU HAD SOMETHING TO DO WITH WHAT HAPPENED.
DO YOU BELIEVE THAT?
DOESN'T MATTER WHAT I BELIEVE.
IT'S AS GOOD AS TRUE.
AND JUDGING BY THE LOOKS OF THAT MOB...
...MARVIN'S NOT ALONE
WELL, I CAN PROVE I HAD NOTHING TO DO WITH IT.
MAYBE EVEN FIND OUT WHO DID.
OH MY!
ASTRA?!

IS THAT REALLY YOU?
WHAT THE HELL ARE YOU DOING WITH THIS eJUNKY?
HE'S TRYING TO HELP ME.
YOU BEST KEEP DREAMING!
ONLY PERSON HECTOR EVER HELPED WAS HIMSELF!
COME ON, COCO.
WE DON'T HAVE MUCH TIME.
IT'S YOUR FUNERAL.

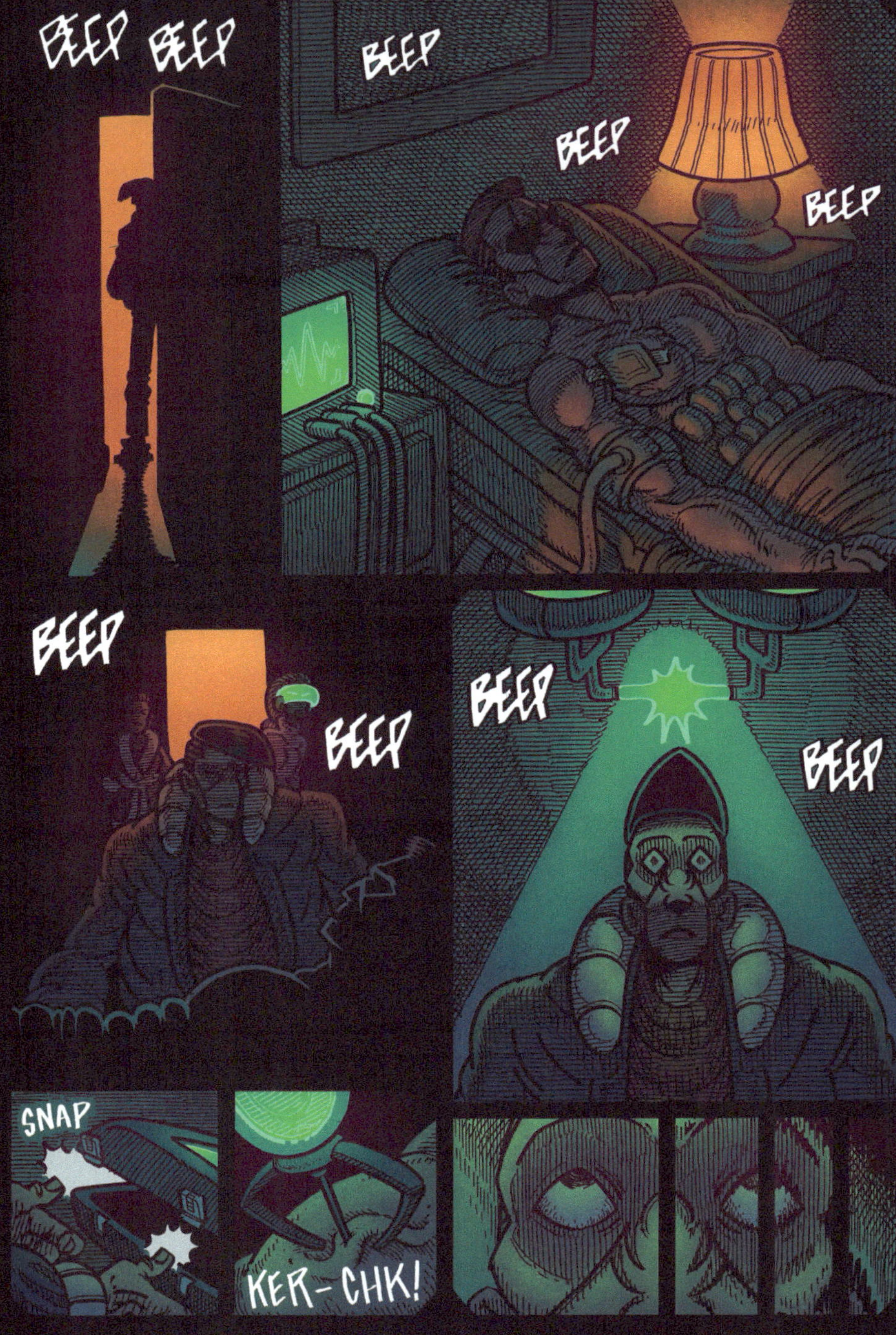

BEEP BEEP
BEEP
BEEP
BEEP
BEEP
BEEP
BEEP
BEEP
BEEP
SNAP
KER-CHK!

CONFESS!
SEPTEMBER 9, 1692. SALEM, MASSACHUSETTS.
GILES COREY.
YOU'RE THROUGH.
CRUSHED.
DEATH IS NIGH.
LOOK!
CONFESS...
...OR YOU WILL BE SENT BACK TO SATAN TO BURN IN HELL.
WHAT DID HE SAY?

ISN'T THAT YOUR BOY?
I THINK HE SAID MORE WEIGHT.
WHAT?
YOHNK
HECTOR?

BANG
BASTARD!
HERE.
THOSE DAMN GUARDIANS SHOT SAMMY!

WE HAVE
TO LEAVE.
NOW!
BAM
AHH!
WAIT!
CAN YOU
CARRY
HIM?
VRG
POP

HELLO!
STOP!
THIS MAN HAD NOTHING TO DO WITH THE ATTACK ON SAM!
BACK OFF!
THESE FOLKS AIN'T YOUR ENEMY!

IT WAS THEM GUARDIANS!
THEY DID SAM WRONG!
HEY!
THEY'RE GETTING AWAY!
OOF!
WHAK
FWMP
COMPUTER, GET US OUT OF HERE!

YOU FOOLS! OUT OF MY WAY!
LET'S SEE WHAT MARVIN HAS TO SAY 'BOUT THIS!
BEEP BEEP BEEP
PATH OBSTRUCTED
COMPUTER, SWITCH TO MANUAL!

THA-
THUMP-A
I SAW
MYSELF. I
WAS THERE.
I KNOW.
I SAW
IT TOO.

I CALLED THEM. YOU WERE IN BAD SHAPE.
HELLO, HECTOR HOLMES.
I'M MELODY ROGERS. A.R.I.S. ORIENTATION SPECIALIST.
WELCOME HOME, MR. HOLMES.
GOOD THING TOO.
YOU SUFFERED A MEMORY CRASH. FRAGMEFLOODING.
TOO MANY ALTERNATIVE EXPERIENCES.
I'VE DONE ALL I CAN.
HE'LL NEED TO TAKE IT EASY FOR A FEW DAYS.
AS A FORMER A.R.I.S., HE'S ENTITLED TO OUR SERVICES, TWENTY-FOUR SEVEN.
DON'T HESITATE TO CONTACT US.

WHY MUST HE CONVALESCE HERE?
HE RISKED HIS LIFE TO HELP ME.
BAM
I DON'T TRUST HIM.
YOU DON'T TRUST ANYONE.
YOU DON'T UNDERSTAND THE WORLD, ASTRA.
I'M BEGINNING TO.
I-I...
I...
...KNOW YOU FROM SOMEWHERE.

CLK
CLK
CLK
CLAK
CLAK
CLAK
CLAK
CLA
DOCTOR PAGAN!
OVER HERE!
CLAK
CLAK
CLAK
CLAK
CLAK
CLAK
CLAK

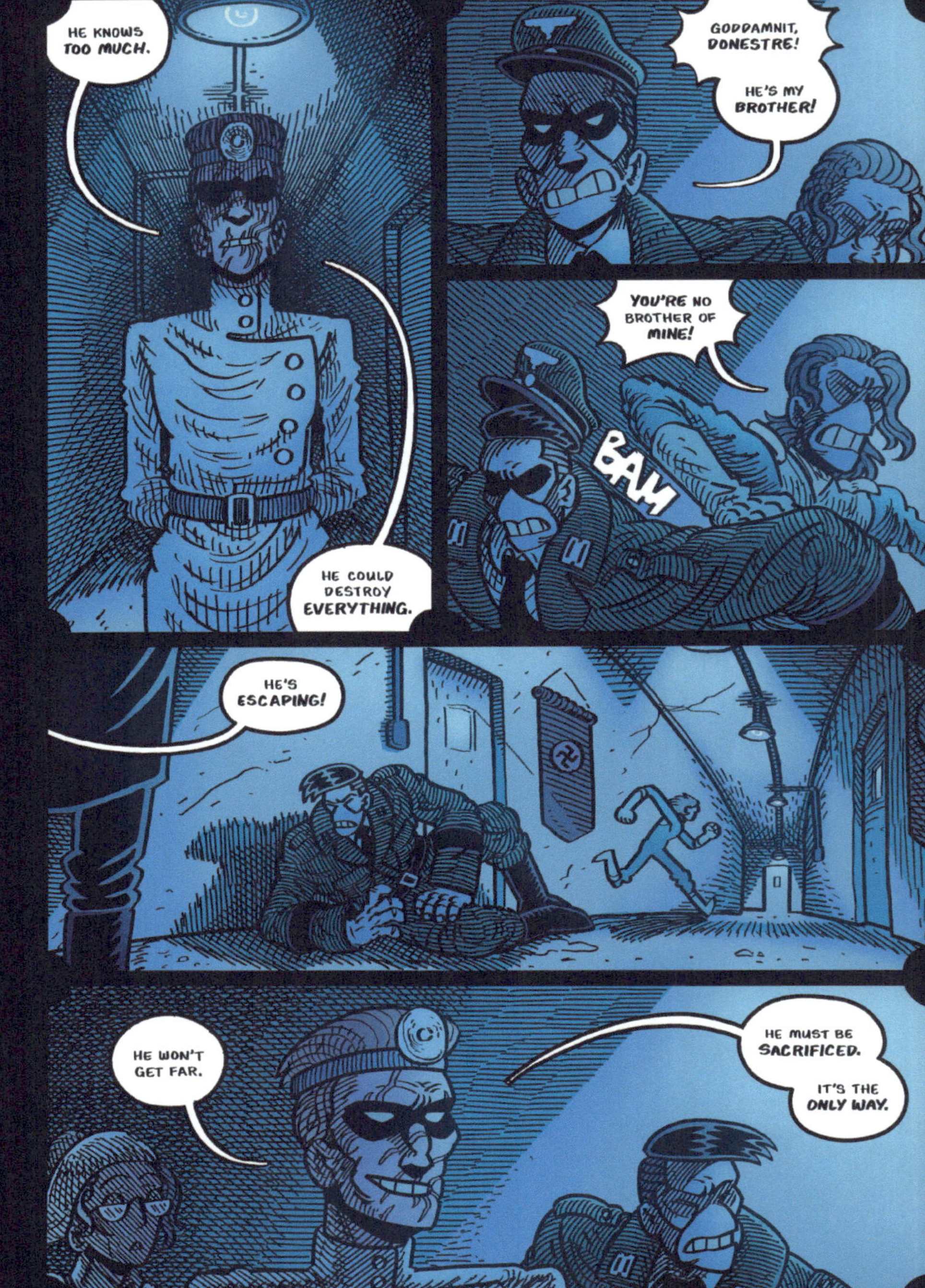

HE KNOWS TOO MUCH.
GODDAMNIT, DONESTRE!
HE'S MY BROTHER!
YOU'RE NO BROTHER OF MINE!
BAM
HE COULD DESTROY EVERYTHING.
HE'S ESCAPING!
HE WON'T GET FAR.
HE MUST BE SACRIFICED.
IT'S THE ONLY WAY.

ARE YOU OKAY?
YOU WERE HAVING A NIGHTMARE.
IT FELT SO REAL! THEY WERE GOING TO KILL MY BROTHER.
MELODY WAS THERE TOO.
SHE SAID YOU WOULD BE CONFUSED.
THESE TORCH EXPERIENCES. PEOPLE APPEARING IN THEM FROM REAL LIFE.
AND NOW THIS DREAM TOO.
I DON'T UNDERSTAND.
DREAMS ARE THE ONE THING I DO UNDERSTAND.
THEY'RE TRYING TO TELL YOU SOMETHING.
HAND ME MY COMPUTER!
BOOP

COMPUTER, SEARCH DOCTOR DONESTRE PAGAN.
DOCTOR DONESTRE PAGAN: FAMED SCIENTIST AND INVENTOR WHO DEDICATED HIMSELF TO THE STUDY OF PAIN AND MEMORY.
BROTHER OF CHRISTIAN PAGAN, A SUCCESSFUL ENTERTAINMENT PRODUCER.
PARADISE LOST
DOCTOR DONESTRE PAGAN SUFFERED FROM A RARE CONGENITAL DISORDER CALLED C.I.P.-- CONGENITAL ANALGESIA, WHICH CAUSED HIM TO FEEL NO PAIN.
THIS INSPIRED HIM TO CREATE THE DRUG EXTRANOL.
EXTRANOL
HE USED HIS DRUG TO EXTRACT BAD MEMORIES WHICH HELPED TO ALLEVIATE HIS CHILDHOOD SUFFERING.
IT LED TO A SERIES OF DISFIGURING SCARS AND SURGERIES THAT LEFT HIM EMOTIONALLY DAMAGED AS WELL.
DOCTOR PAGAN SOLD HIS PATENT TO THE W.C.O. IN 2037...

...BUT TRAGEDY STRUCK AFTER HE BECAME MENTALLY UNSTABLE AND HAD TO BE INSTITUTIONALIZED...
...AT THE L.A. CENTER FOR BEHAVIORAL AND PSYCHIATRIC STUDIES.
DO YOU THINK DONESTRE COULD BE BEHIND THE GUARDIANS?
NO.
MORE INFO
HE'S DEAD.
DONESTRE PAGAN DIES WHILE STILL A PATIENT AT THE L.A. CENTER FOR BEHAVIORAL AND PSYCHIATRIC STUDIES.
MORE
THESIS ON DNA SCRAPING FOR CELLMEM PRESERVATION.
AUTHOR: DR. PAGAN, DR. EMORY
READ
I THINK I'LL CHECK OUT THIS DR. EMORY.
SWWP

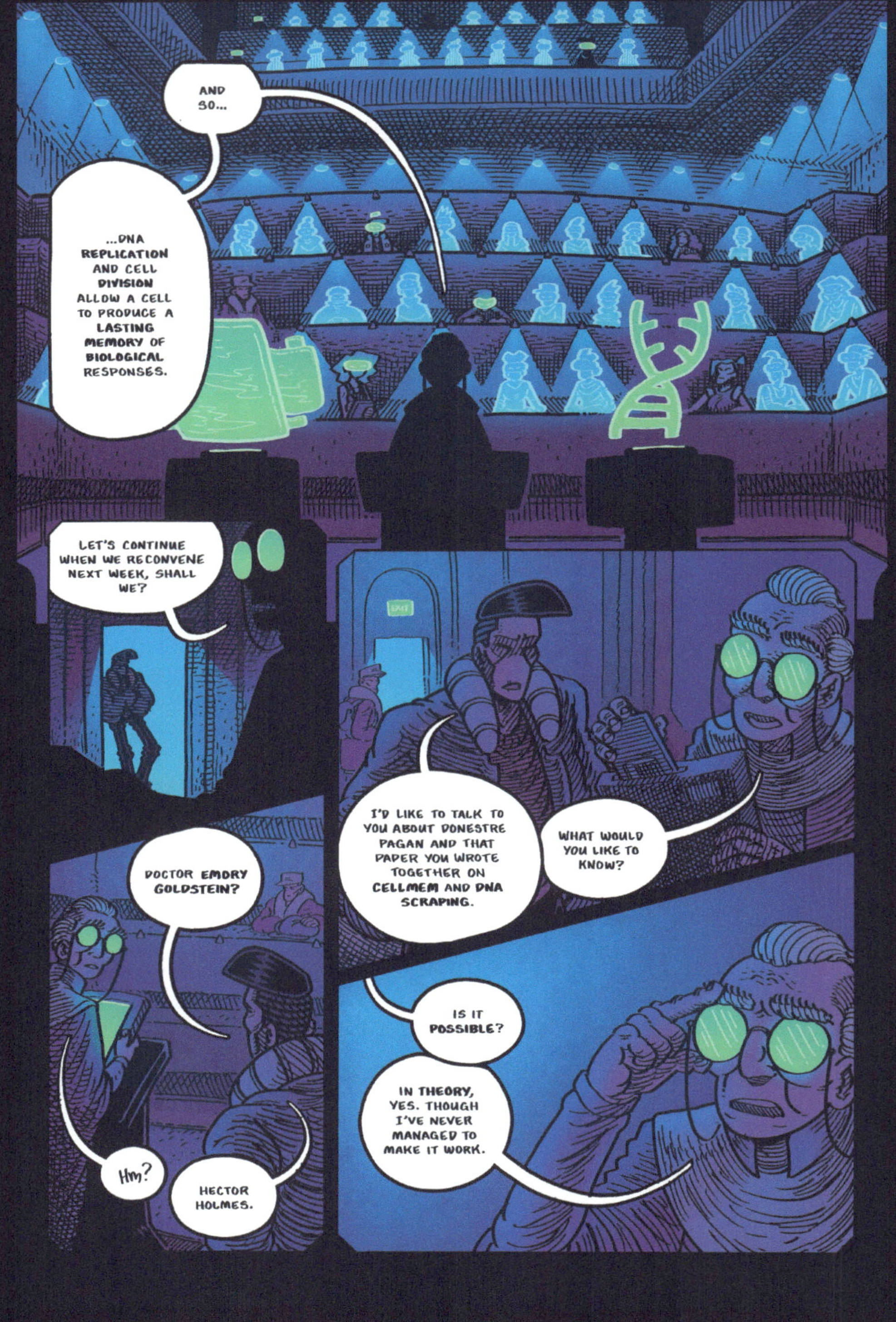

AND SO...
...DNA REPLICATION AND CELL DIVISION ALLOW A CELL TO PRODUCE A LASTING MEMORY OF BIOLOGICAL RESPONSES.
LET'S CONTINUE WHEN WE RECONVENE NEXT WEEK, SHALL WE?
DOCTOR EMDRY GOLDSTEIN?
I'D LIKE TO TALK TO YOU ABOUT DONESTRE PAGAN AND THAT PAPER YOU WROTE TOGETHER ON CELLMEM AND DNA SCRAPING.
WHAT WOULD YOU LIKE TO KNOW?
IS IT POSSIBLE?
IN THEORY, YES. THOUGH I'VE NEVER MANAGED TO MAKE IT WORK.
HM?
HECTOR HOLMES.

CELLS DIE.
EVEN WHEN THE CELLMEM IS FROZEN RIGHT AWAY, IT DECAYS.
THIS TORCH THAT'S ALL OVER THE NEWS?
IF IT WORKS, IT WOULD BE A MIRACLE.
DO YOU THINK DONESTRE COULD HAVE BEEN SOMEHOW BEHIND ITS CREATION?
HE'S CERTAINLY CAPABLE. BUT HE BECAME OBSESSED WITH HIS DRUG EXTRANOL--
--I LOST TOUCH WITH HIM AFTER THAT.
WHEN DID YOU LAST SPEAK TO HIM?
OH, IT'S BEEN YEARS.
CALLED ME UP PARANOID THAT THE W.C.O. WAS TRYING TO KILL HIM.
THEN, HE SOLD THE PATENT TO THEM FOR BILLIONS.
NEXT THING I HEARD...

"...HE WAS ADMITTED AS A PATIENT TO THE L.A. CENTER FOR BEHAVIORAL AND PSYCHIATRIC STUDIES.
"TWO MONTHS LATER, HE WAS DEAD."
BEHAVIORAL & PSYCHIATRIC STUDIES
GREETINGS, MR. HOLMES.
HOW MIGHT I ASSIST YOU?
I'D LIKE ALL PATIENT RECORDS ON DONESTRE PAGAN.
I'M SORRY, YOU'RE NOT AUTHORIZED. PATIENT RECORDS ARE CONFIDENTIAL.
CONTACT A.R.I.S. INVESTIGATOR MIKE MILLER. HE'LL AUTHORIZE MY ACCESS.
CHK WHIRRRR BEEP
ACCESS APPROVED. PATIENT RECORD 666.34.49.
CAN YOU GIVE ME A COPY OF THE DEATH CERTIFICATE?
NEGATIVE. THERE IS NO DEATH CERTIFICATE ON FILE.
HOW IS THAT POSSIBLE?
I CANNOT ANSWER THAT QUESTION AT THIS TIME.

IS THERE SOMEONE HERE WHO COULD?
ANYONE WHO CAN VERIFY HE WAS A PATIENT HERE?
ANYONE WHO TREATED HIM?
THERE IS ONE.
DOCTOR CASSANDRA MOORE. CLINICAL PSYCHIATRIST.
SO THE ONLY PERSON WHO CAN VERIFY DONESTRE PAGAN IS DEAD, IS IN A COMA?
AFFIRMATIVE.
ANY NEXT OF KIN?
CHK- WHIRRR
CHK CHK WHIRR
BEEP
DONESTRE PAGAN'S ONLY EMERGENCY CONTACT WAS HIS BROTHER CHRISTIAN PAGAN.

SO, YOU THINK DONESTRE FAKED HIS DEATH?
IT'S POSSIBLE.
I'M HOPING TO MEET WITH HIS BROTHER NEXT.
CHRISTIAN PAGAN.

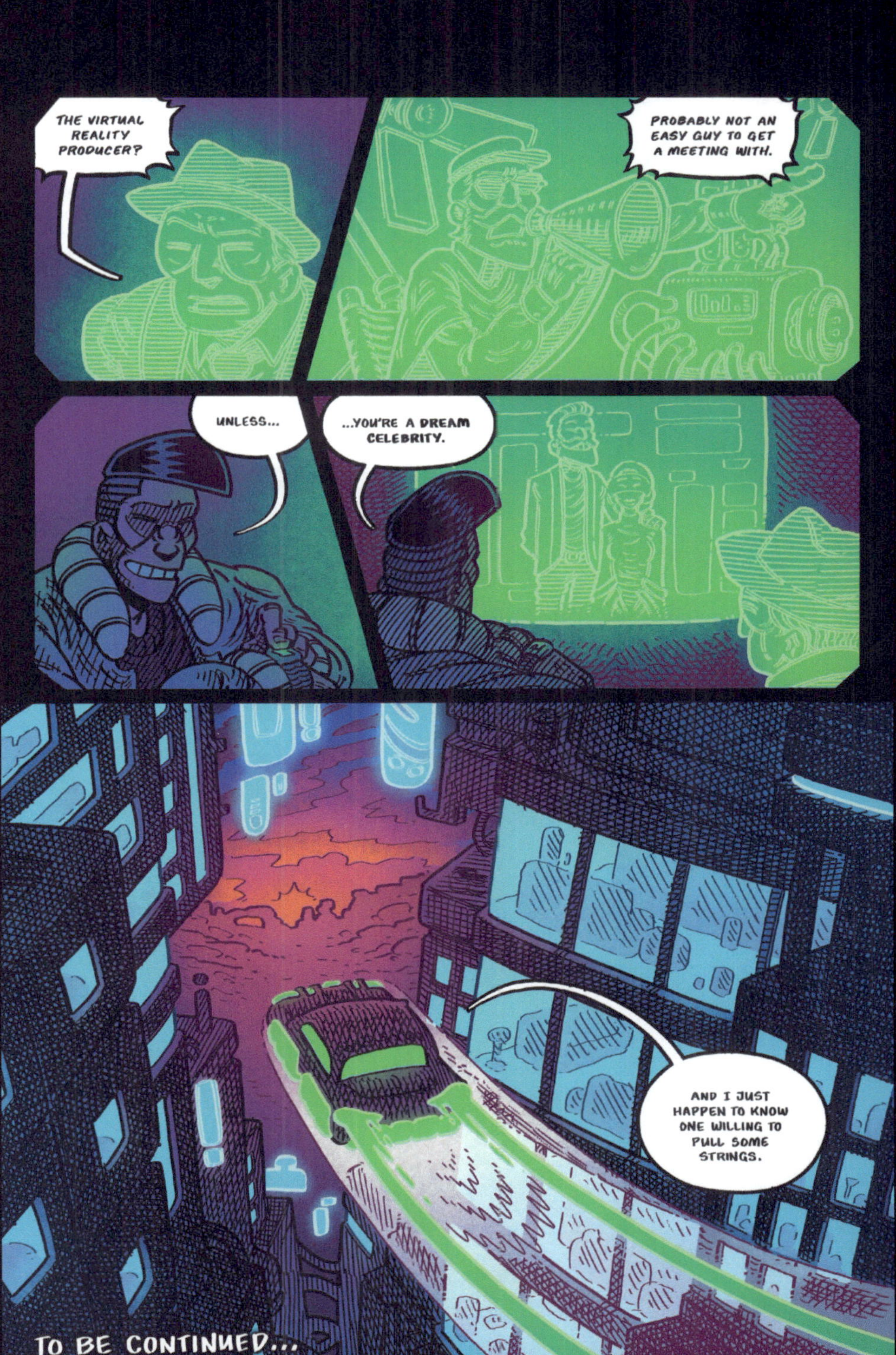

THE VIRTUAL REALITY PRODUCER?
PROBABLY NOT AN EASY GUY TO GET A MEETING WITH.
UNLESS...
...YOU'RE A DREAM CELEBRITY.
AND I JUST HAPPEN TO KNOW ONE WILLING TO PULL SOME STRINGS.
TO BE CONTINUED...

NRD
™


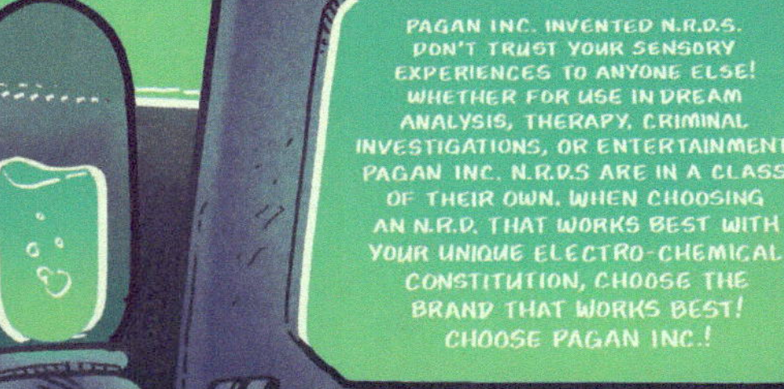

PAGAN INC.'S PATENTED NERVE READING DEVICES (N.R.D.S) PROVIDE SUPERIOR QUALITY IN SENSORY PROJECTION.

FROM THE MEGA DELUXE MODELS USED BY DREAM CELEBRITIES TO CAPTURE THE VIVIDNESS AND SURREALISM OF THEIR DREAMWORLDS TO THE USE OF THE PORTABLE MINISYNCH MODELS FOR RECORDING, SHARING, AND PROJECTING EXPERIENCES WHILE TRAVELING, OUR NERVE READING DEVICES OFFER UNMATCHED QUALITY AT AN AFFORDABLE PRICE.

FEATURES AND BENEFITS

○ RECYCLED TITANIUM, LIFETIME-DURABILITY SEAL ENSURES OUR N.R.D.S LAST OR YOUR MONEY BACK

○ TETRATONIC SENSORY SEALS TO PREVENT DREAM HACKS AND SENSORY DEGRADATION TO GUARANTEE VIBRANT, PURE, AND AUTHENTIC EXPERIENCES.

○ BUILT-IN, SUBCUTANEOUS SEQUENCING PROVIDES MORE ACCURATE SENSORY PERCEPTION

○ EASY-TO-NAVIGATE INTERFACE PROVIDES FULL CONTROL OVER YOUR PREVIEWS

PAGAN INC. INVENTED N.R.D.S. DON'T TRUST YOUR SENSORY EXPERIENCES TO ANYONE ELSE! WHETHER FOR USE IN DREAM ANALYSIS, THERAPY, CRIMINAL INVESTIGATIONS, OR ENTERTAINMENT, PAGAN INC. N.R.D.S ARE IN A CLASS OF THEIR OWN. WHEN CHOOSING AN N.R.D. THAT WORKS BEST WITH YOUR UNIQUE ELECTRO-CHEMICAL CONSTITUTION, CHOOSE THE BRAND THAT WORKS BEST! CHOOSE PAGAN INC.!

PAGAN INC

P.A.T.
MANIFESTO

OUR MOTTO
THE TRUTH WILL SET YOU FREE!

OUR MISSION
TO USE EVERY LEGAL MEASURE POSSIBLE TO PRESERVE LIFE WHILE PROTECTING THE ENVIRONMENT AND ITS INHABITANTS FROM THE ABUSE OF TECHNOLOGY.

OUR MEMBERS
PEOPLE AGAINST TECHNOLOGY (P.A.T.) WAS ORIGINALLY FOUNDED IN 2039 BY HORUS KHALED, BEHAVIORAL PSYCHOLOGIST AND BUDDHIST MONK, AND DONESTRE PAGAN, RENOWNED INVENTOR, SCIENTIST, AND FOUNDER OF PAGAN INC. P.A.T. NOW INCLUDES THOUSANDS OF FREE MEMBERS WHO VOW TO WORK TIRELESSLY TO DEFEND THE FREEDOMS AND INTERESTS OF ALL SENTIENT BEINGS WITH WHOM WE SHARE THIS UNIVERSE.

OUR BELIEFS
P.A.T. BELIEVES FIRMLY AND PASSIONATELY IN THE FOLLOWING:

o TECHNOLOGY SHOULD SERVE PEOPLE, NOT THE OTHER WAY AROUND
o TECHNOLOGY USED TO CONTROL PEOPLE IS A THREAT TO OUR SURVIVAL
o TECHNOLOGY OFTEN DOES MORE HARM THAN GOOD FOR THE ENVIRONMENT
o TECHNOLOGY OFTEN DIMINISHES THE QUALITY OF OUR RELATIONSHIPS
o MAKING TECHNOLOGY MANDATORY DESTROYS OUR FREEDOMS, HOPES, AND DREAMS
o LIFE EXPERIENCES ARE RENDERED LESS PURE THROUGH TECHNOLOGY
o PEOPLE MUST FIGHT DAILY TO END THE ABUSE OF TECHNOLOGY

## INTRODUCTION

DNA replication and cell division allow a cell to produce a lasting memory of biological responses.

Memory was once believed to be stored on the cellular level in the synapses. This memory was believed to get passed from one cell to another synaptically. As studies evolved, science revealed that storage of both short-term and long-term memory was preserved within the nucleus of the cell.

In 2027, radical discoveries were made by Rowdy J. Schwarman. The oft-cited Stanford biologist studied the memory of rats and determined that storage could be found within the DNA. Schwarman proved definitively that after destroying all traces of memory within the synapses that the memory could be regenerated from DNA extracted from blood. (1) To extend the half-life of the memory, the sample must be stored with a mixture of preservation compounds immediately following extraction, a crucial discovery made by Cal George and Gregory Blair. (2)

In time, techniques evolved to record and experience this memory. We are thinking especially of Schwarman's studies which proved memories could be recorded and experienced through intravenously sharing the DNA with intraperitoneally applied arginine/DNA complexes absorbed into the systemic circulation and distributed to the major organs. (1)

Of course, the studies of G.B. Tamarind showed that the process of extracting memories resulted in a more real, vivid experience when the cellular memory of the experience was extracted and sampled within 10 days of the memory being formed. (3)

DNA scraping techniques have evolved recently, however, to increase the time before memories begin to decay from 10 days to 30 days.

Recent tests using advanced techniques in bone scraping have proven challenging. Memory loss beyond 30 days is significant, despite the numerous efforts by Michael J. Florio and Summer Suleiman to preserve the experiences. (4) In theory, however, modern DNA scraping techniques using the right chemical reagent can be applied to preserve these memories indefinitely, allowing for the DNA scraping of corpses dating back centuries, as postulated by Cassandra D'Agosta. (5)

There is no reason why the preservation of cellular memory cannot be made possible through the introduction of various reagents and chemical compounds that would help to replicate missing experiences and restore memory degradation.

The results of such experiences would be equivalent to a first-generation experience and could also, in theory, avoid the typical deterioration and mutation in most DNA after 30 days.

In summary, if applied properly, this could allow people to experience what it would be like to have lived as a primordial human. This would undoubtedly make historic experiences as vivid as yesterday's memory to the person dosing Alternative Reality experiences extracted from corpses dating back thousands of years.

## REFERENCES

1. ROWDY J. SCHWARMAN. (2032). INTRACELLULAR PRESERVATION TECHNIQUES USING BIOLOGICALLY ACTIVE PROTEINS, COMPOUNDS AND DNA. BIOSSOURCE TECH. 2000;21:45--48. DOI: 10.1016/S0165-6147(99)01479-7.

2. CAL W. GEORGE, GREGORY BLAIR. (2032). EXTENDING HALF-LIFE AND PRESERVING CELLMEM EXTRACTION SAMPLES. HEMATOLOGICAL REVIEW. 2000;19:003--621. DOI 40.1595/J.RIFAC.3476.10.508.

3. G.B. TAMARIND (2032). A HISTORY OF CELL MEMORY PRESERVATION. SCIENCE SOURCE REV. 1005;44:637--321. DOI: 10.1116/J.ADPR.2003.99.002.

4. MICHAEL J. FLORIO, SUMMER SULEIMAN. (2032). IMPEDING AND PREVENTING CELLMEM DECAY BEYOND 30 DAYS. FRONTIERS IN CELLULAR BIOLOGY. 3313;54:882--332. DOI: 99.2022/S.FTHC.71.2.651.

5. CASSANDRA M. D'AGOSTA. (2033). CHEMICAL REAGENTS FOR DNA PRESERVATION. NATL ACAD SCI USA. 2024;91:664--668. DOI: 08.1072/PNAS.71.2.651.

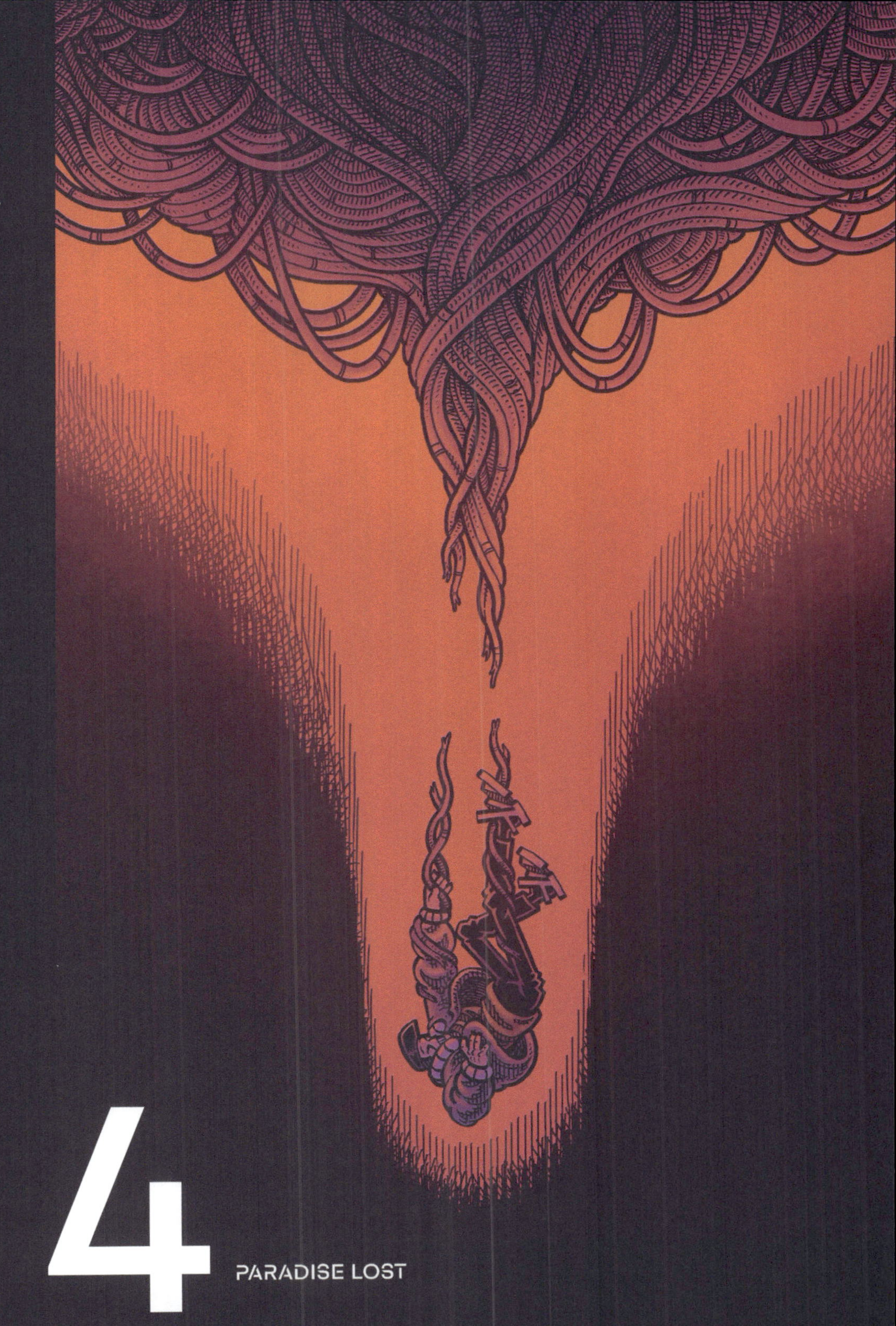

4
PARADISE LOST

# CHAPTER 4

HECTOR?!
WHAT ARE YOU DOING HERE?
LOOKING FOR CHRISTIAN PAGAN.
OH, ASTRA. THIS IS DESIRAE. SHE'S AN ACTRESS.
YES, A REAL ONE.
WELL, I BETTER GET BACK TO WORK. YOU'LL FIND MR. PAGAN'S OFFICE OVER THERE.

HOW DO YOU KNOW HER?
ANCIENT HISTORY.
SHE'S VERY FRIENDLY.
DIRECTOR CHRISTIAN PAGAN
"ABASHED THE DEVIL STOOD AND FELT HOW AWFUL GOODNESS IS AND SAW VIRTUE IN HER SHAPE HOW LOVELY--SAW, AND PINED HIS LOSS."

A PASSAGE FROM MY FAVORITE WORK. MILTON'S PARADISE LOST.
IT DESCRIBES THE DEVIL'S MINDSET. NOW WHY WOULD THE ANGEL OF LIGHT REGARD GOODNESS AS AWFUL?
FUNNY. I'VE NEVER HEARD THE DEVIL REFERRED TO AS THE ANGEL OF LIGHT.
1
2
YES, HE WAS. BEFORE HIS FALL.
IRONIC, ISN'T IT?
ARE THESE BOOKS? DO YOU MIND IF I LOOK?
3
BE MY GUEST.
4
NO EMO-REG, MR. PAGAN?
I'VE LEARNED TO LIVE BY MY OWN RULES.
SNAP
AND WHAT WOULD SHOW BUSINESS BE WITHOUT FEELINGS?

THESE BOOKS-- WHAT ARE THEY FOR?
RELICS.
CONTAINING MISSING HISTORY.
DO YOU ENJOY WHAT YOU DO, MR. PAGAN?
I DO.
WHAT HISTORY?
WHY, HISTORY RELATED TO OUR WORK, MR. HOLMES.
PRODUCING HISTORICAL RE-ENACTMENTS TO BE VIEWED AS VIRTUAL REALITY IS WHAT WE DO HERE.
BUT IT'S HARD AS OF LATE.
WELL, AS THE SAYING GOES, "ALL THE WORLD'S A STAGE."
BUT THAT'S NOT WHY YOU'RE HERE. IS IT, MR. HOLMES?
THE W.C.O. REGULATES WHAT WE CAN PERFORM AND WHEN.
ANYTHING TOO OFFENSIVE, WHICH MIGHT CAUSE SUFFERING, MUST BE ERASED.
IT'S A SHAME REALLY. FEELS PHONY.
MORE LIKE ENTERTAINMENT THAN EDUCATION.
IS THERE A DIFFERENCE?

SO IF YOU'D PLEASE, GET TO THE POINT.
WE'RE INVESTIGATING YOUR BROTHER DONESTRE.
MY BROTHER'S DEAD.
ARE YOU SURE? WHEN I CHECKED PATIENT RECORDS, THERE WAS NO DEATH CERTIFICATE.
AND THE ONLY PERSON STILL WORKING AT THE HOSPITAL WHO MIGHT HAVE RECALLED WORKING WITH YOUR BROTHER IS IN A COMA. EVERYONE ELSE IS DEAD.
WHAT ARE YOU IMPLYING?
I THINK IT'S POSSIBLE YOUR BROTHER FAKED HIS DEATH AND HAD ALL THOSE PEOPLE KILLED TO COVER IT UP.
VERY SHAKESPEAREAN, BUT RIDICULOUS!
WHY WOULD HE DO THAT?
I SHOULD HIRE YOU HERE AS ONE OF MY WRITERS.
YOUR IMAGINATION IMPRESSES ME!
BECAUSE NO ONE WOULD EVER SUSPECT A DEAD MAN OF BEING THE LEADER OF THE GUARDIANS.
WHAT ON EARTH MAKES YOU THINK THAT?
THE RADICAL PAPERS HE PUBLISHED ON CELLMEM PRESERVATION AND EXTRACTION. A THEORY THAT WAS PROVEN THROUGH TORCH.
REALLY, MR. HOLMES?
BLAMING MY DEAD BROTHER FOR TORCH?

YOU MIGHT AS WELL BLAME ASTRA FOR WHAT HAPPENED AT HEAVEN'S HALL.
WELL... HOPEFULLY THEY'RE IN A BETTER PLACE NOW.
IS THAT WHAT YOU FEEL?
OR WHAT THIS THING TELLS YOU TO FEEL?
MY BROTHER IS DEAD.
AND I'M A BUSY MAN. SO IF THERE'S NOTHING ELSE--
NO, THERE IS SOMETHING ELSE.
AS HIS ONLY LIVING KIN, WE NEED YOUR PERMISSION TO SCRAPE HIS DNA.

YOU WANT TO PROBE MY BROTHER'S CORPSE...
...TO TEST SOME WILD THEORY?
I'M SORRY, I CAN'T AUTHORIZE THAT.
YOU CAN'T, OR YOU WON'T?
I MEAN...IF YOU HAVE NOTHING TO HIDE--
TELL ME SOMETHING, MR. HOLMES.
DO YOU BLAME YOURSELF FOR YOUR BROTHER'S DEATH?
YES, I RESEARCHED YOU, TOO.
STRANGE, HOW HE DIED, WASN'T IT?
LET'S GO!
YOUR PURSUIT OF THE GUARDIANS IS NOT GOING TO BRING YOUR BROTHER BACK!
OR MINE.

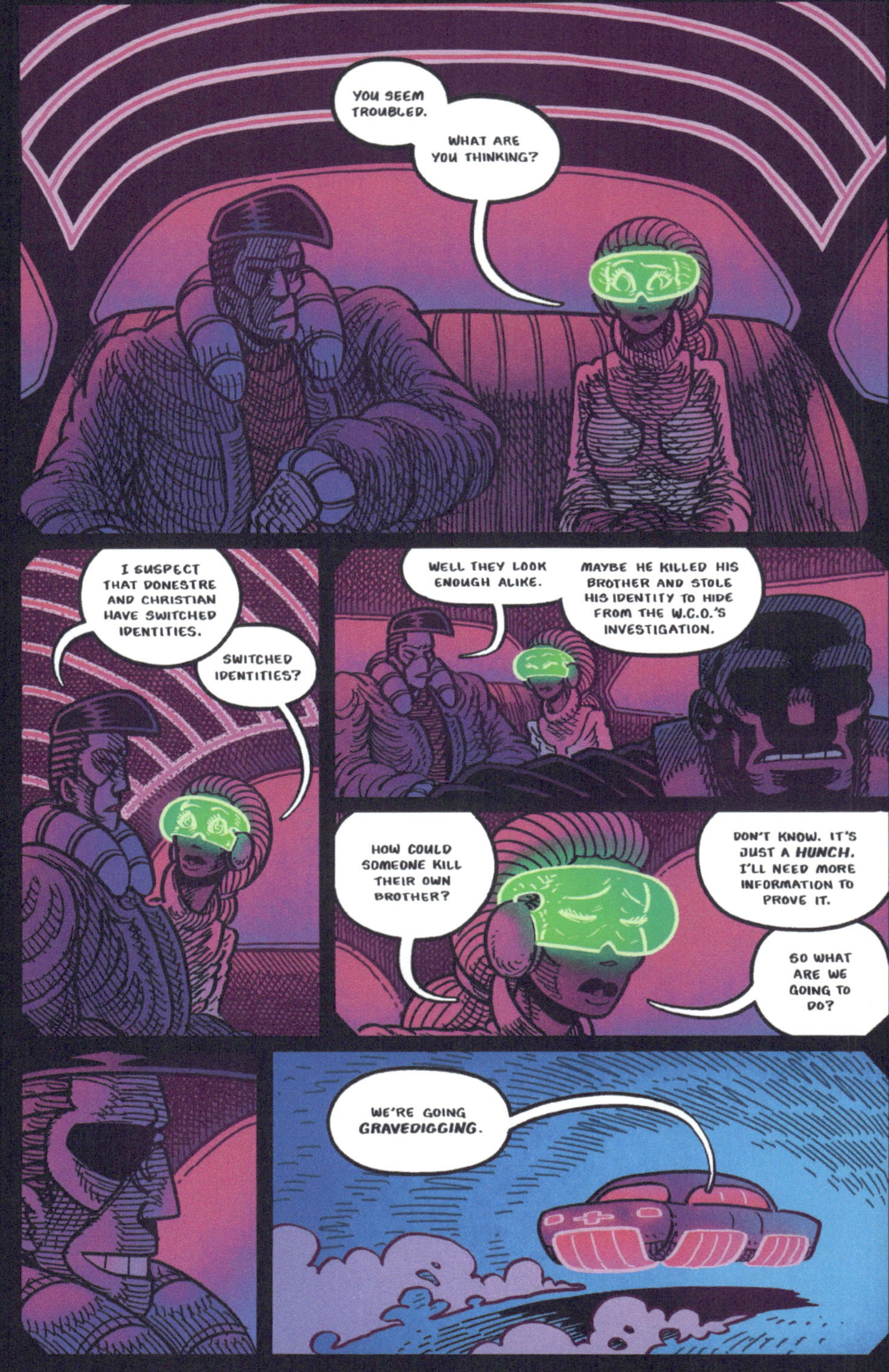

YOU SEEM TROUBLED.
WHAT ARE YOU THINKING?
I SUSPECT THAT DONESTRE AND CHRISTIAN HAVE SWITCHED IDENTITIES.
SWITCHED IDENTITIES?
WELL THEY LOOK ENOUGH ALIKE.
MAYBE HE KILLED HIS BROTHER AND STOLE HIS IDENTITY TO HIDE FROM THE W.C.O.'S INVESTIGATION.
HOW COULD SOMEONE KILL THEIR OWN BROTHER?
DON'T KNOW. IT'S JUST A HUNCH. I'LL NEED MORE INFORMATION TO PROVE IT.
SO WHAT ARE WE GOING TO DO?
WE'RE GOING GRAVEDIGGING.

IT'S SO PEACEFUL.
YOU'RE NOT SCARED?
WHY?
SOMETIMES, I WISH I WERE INNOCENT.
THE CRYPT'S THERE.

LET'S GO.
DOMESTIC PAGAN
HOW ARE WE SUPPOSED TO OPEN IT?

HMPH!
WHAM
CRASH

JONES
PAGAN

CAN YOU HANDLE THIS?
RRRRRR

THUD

SCRAPE
THEY'RE HERE.

WHO?
THE GUARDIANS.
THEY HAVE SUCH INTERESTING MASKS.
TAKE THAT THING OFF!
NOW!
FEAR IS YOUR FRIEND, IF YOU HOPE TO SURVIVE.

WHAT ARE
WE GOING
TO DO?
IT'S
OK.
WE'LL
BE OK.
NOD
SWWOOOSH
SMASH

RRG!
CRACKLE
RAAGH!
GO!
URGH!
RARRGGH!!
WHUMP
TUMULT!

STAY CLOSE.
OOOMPH!
KRAKKT
UUGH!
SHIT!
YEARRGH!
CLANG CLANG CLANG
GRAB HER!
THUD
GRAB
OMMPF!
WHAM

HECTOR!

HELLPP!

?AHHG

SSSSSS
HUFF
HUFF

HMMF

BANG
BANG
BANG
BANG

BANG
BANG
BANG

137

GUH...
NO!
HRRK
HECTOR!
ASTRA!
THOKK
WHMF

GUHHHH...
WHERE AM I?
POOR KID.
GOTTA WAIT FOR MY MOMENT.
KER-CHK
KICK
SLAM

DON'T! OR I'LL KILL HIM!
KHOK
THUD
TRIP
BANG
OOF!

CHK
VVRRRROOOMM
OOOMMMPF!
THMP
THUD
AGAINST THE WALL!
I SAID-- GO FASTER!
FASTER!
WHAT?
VMMMM

YANK
TORIN! WHY?
I'M SORRY. I WAS NEVER GOING TO LET THEM HURT YOU.
HONK HONK
WRRDOOMM
BEEP BEEP BEEP
HE'LL BLOW US UP!
GET OUT!
00:09

HUP!
AHHHHH
BROOM

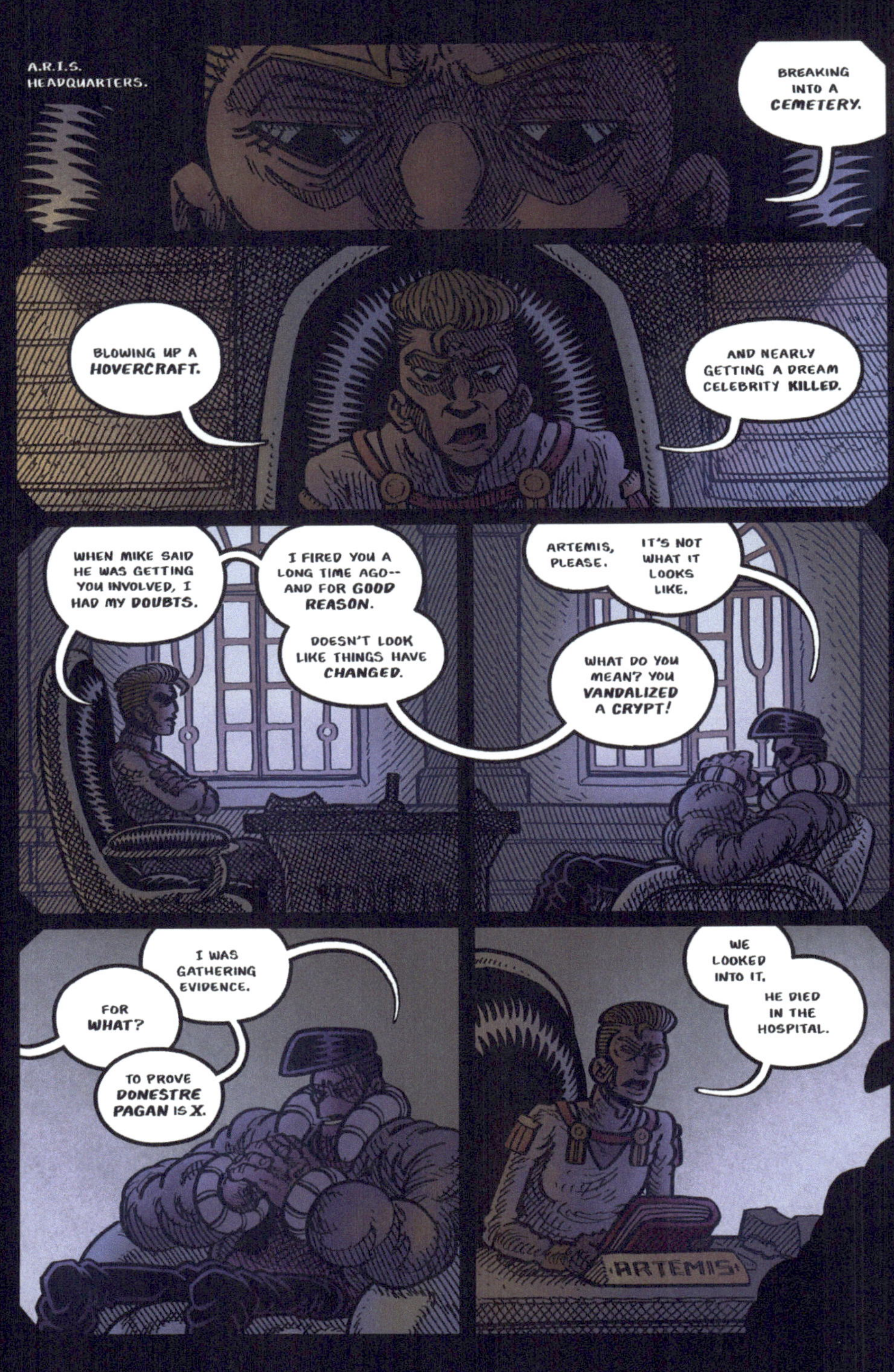

A.R.I.S. HEADQUARTERS.
BREAKING INTO A CEMETERY.
BLOWING UP A HOVERCRAFT.
AND NEARLY GETTING A DREAM CELEBRITY KILLED.
WHEN MIKE SAID HE WAS GETTING YOU INVOLVED, I HAD MY DOUBTS.
I FIRED YOU A LONG TIME AGO-- AND FOR GOOD REASON.
DOESN'T LOOK LIKE THINGS HAVE CHANGED.
ARTEMIS, PLEASE.
IT'S NOT WHAT IT LOOKS LIKE.
WHAT DO YOU MEAN? YOU VANDALIZED A CRYPT!
I WAS GATHERING EVIDENCE.
FOR WHAT?
TO PROVE DONESTRE PAGAN IS X.
WE LOOKED INTO IT. HE DIED IN THE HOSPITAL.
ARTEMIS

BUT EVERYONE WHO COULD IDENTIFY DONESTRE IS DEAD TOO!
EXCEPT CASSANDRA MOORE, AND SHE'S IN A COMA!
SO HE FAKED HIS DEATH?
THINK ABOUT IT! IT'S THE ULTIMATE ALIBI!
WE HAVE TO GET THAT DNA CHECKED!
IT'S NO LONGER "WE".
YOU ARE NO LONGER A PART OF THIS ORGANIZATION. IN FACT, I DON'T KNOW IF YOU EVER WERE.
SLAM
I'M GLAD YOU BROUGHT UP DR. MOORE.
<N.R.O.>
PRGAN INC.
WE'RE GOING TO HAVE TO ARREST YOU.
I BELIEVE THIS IS YOURS.
FOR WHAT?!
ACCORDING TO THE VISITOR LOG, YOU WENT TO THE HOSPITAL TO VISIT DOCTOR MOORE ON A NUMBER OF OCCASIONS.
ON DATES THAT CORRESPOND EXACTLY WITH WHEN THOSE CHEMICALS WERE TAKEN.

THIS FOOTAGE IS FROM SIX MONTHS AGO.
RESUME PLAYBACK
CLIK
REC
REC
REC
REC
THAT VIDEO WAS OBVIOUSLY FAKED!
OUR ANALYSTS CHECKED IT OUT. NO TAMPERING.
ARE YOU WORKING WITH THE GUARDIANS, HECTOR HOLMES?
IF I WERE, WHY WOULD I BE TRYING TO HAND OVER EVIDENCE?!

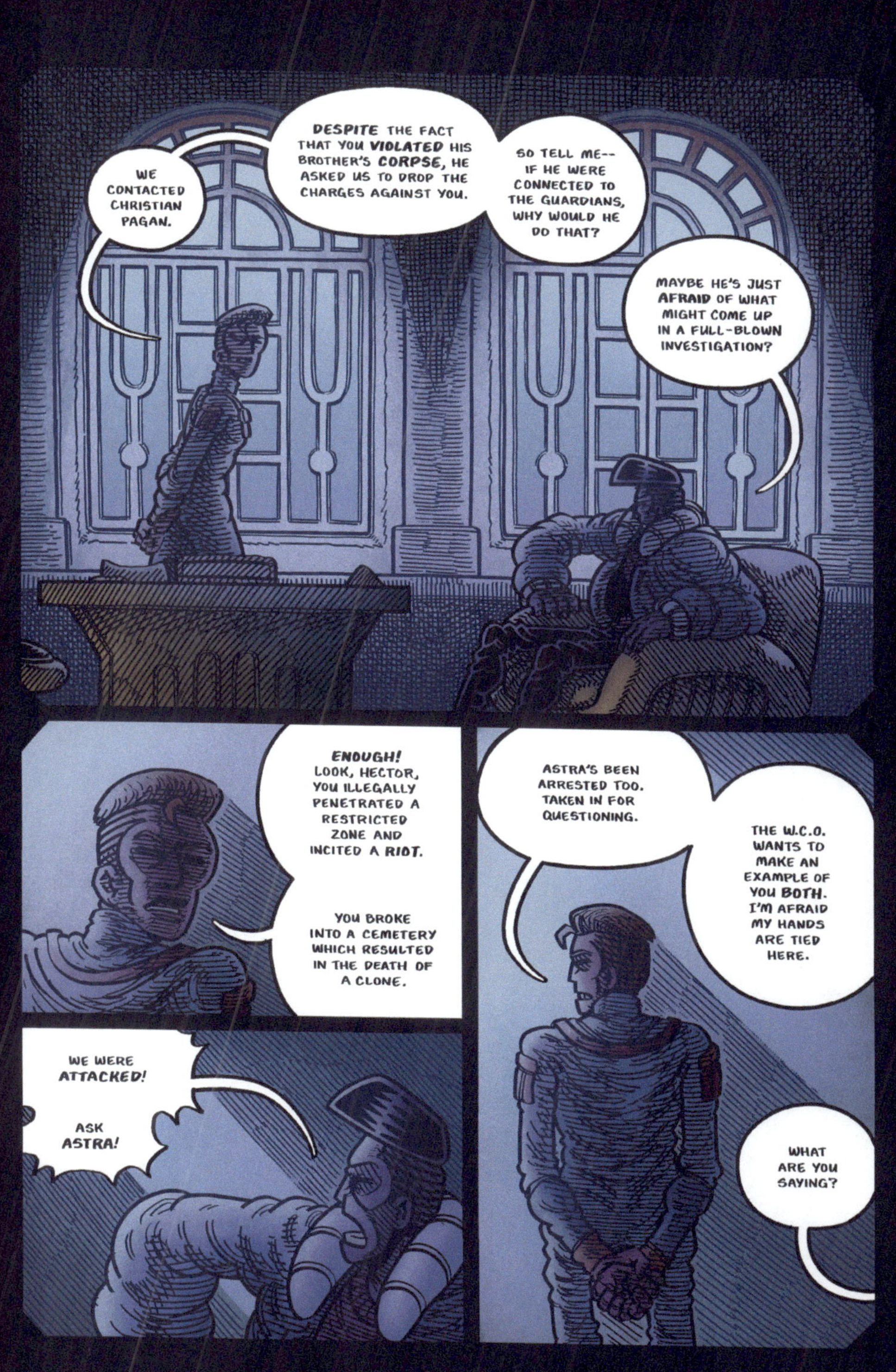

WE CONTACTED CHRISTIAN PAGAN.
DESPITE THE FACT THAT YOU VIOLATED HIS BROTHER'S CORPSE, HE ASKED US TO DROP THE CHARGES AGAINST YOU.
SO TELL ME-- IF HE WERE CONNECTED TO THE GUARDIANS, WHY WOULD HE DO THAT?
MAYBE HE'S JUST AFRAID OF WHAT MIGHT COME UP IN A FULL-BLOWN INVESTIGATION?
ENOUGH! LOOK, HECTOR, YOU ILLEGALLY PENETRATED A RESTRICTED ZONE AND INCITED A RIOT.
YOU BROKE INTO A CEMETERY WHICH RESULTED IN THE DEATH OF A CLONE.
ASTRA'S BEEN ARRESTED TOO. TAKEN IN FOR QUESTIONING.
THE W.C.O. WANTS TO MAKE AN EXAMPLE OF YOU BOTH. I'M AFRAID MY HANDS ARE TIED HERE.
WE WERE ATTACKED!
ASK ASTRA!
WHAT ARE YOU SAYING?

ASTRA WILL LIKELY GET OFF WITH SOME COMMUNITY SERVICE...
...BUT YOU?
--YOU'RE GETTING YOUR MEMORY SCRAPED FOR EVERY DETAIL TO FIND OUT WHATEVER YOU KNOW THAT YOU'RE NOT TELLING.
AND THEN, YOU'RE GOING TO BE PUT AWAY FOR A VERY LONG TIME.
I'M SORRY, HECTOR. I REALLY AM.
FIRST YOUR BROTHER AND NOW YOU.
I WISH I KNEW WHERE THINGS WENT WRONG.

NO!
YOU BASTARDS!
SLAM

YANK
TOXIRHNOL

I CAN HANDLE IT FROM HERE.

HELLO,
HECTOR.
SLAM
BEEP
BEEP
BEEP
BEEP
BEEP
AUSCHWITZ, POLAND.
NOVEMBER, 1943.
BEEP BEEP
BPM
BEEP BEEP

IT WON'T WORK!
THE MEMORY WIPE.
AND I THINK YOU KNOW IT.
DON'T YOU?
I KNOW.
THIS WAS FOR SHOW.
YOUR MEMORY WAS ERASED TO ELIMINATE INCRIMINATING EVIDENCE.
IT WAS SUPPOSED TO LAST FOREVER.
BUT IT DIDN'T.
BEEP
BEEP
BEEP
SIGH
BEEP

AFTER YOU DOSED TORCH, THE EFFECTS WERE SOMEHOW REVERSED.
PAST EXPERIENCES CAME FLOODING BACK.
NOW, I'M AFRAID, YOUR MEMORIES WILL BE USED AGAINST YOU.
AGAINST US ALL.
BEEP
BEEP
THAT'S WHY...
BEEP
...I'M GOING TO HELP YOU ESCAPE.
BEEP

SO FAR, SO GOOD.
SPOKE TOO SOON!
zzzip
WHAT THE--
WAIT!
IT'S OK!
KLIK

HE'S WITH ME!
SUCKER!
TAKE HIS GUN.
YOU'LL NEED IT.
HEY!
POP
POP
POP POP
POP

"STICK
TO THE
PLAN.

"THE HOVER-
CRAFT WILL
BE WAITING
OUT BACK."

ARTEMIS + CHIEF + INVESTIGATOR

REPORT

DON'T DO THIS, HECTOR.
YOU'LL NEVER GET AWAY WITH IT.
I'M NOT TRYING TO GET AWAY WITH ANYTHING!
I'M TRYING TO MAKE THINGS RIGHT!
HECTOR, DON'T!
BAM

I HAVE TO!
I NEED TO KNOW THE TRUTH.

THUD
OOP.
SHALE FRAK!
WHMP

TO BE CONCLUDED...

EXTRANOL

FORGET WHAT YOU WANT.
REMEMBER WHAT YOU NEED.

WITH EXTRANOL, YOU CAN STAY POSITIVE
WHILE FORGETTING THE NEGATIVE. EXTRANOL
IS SCIENTIFICALLY PROVEN TO BE EFFECTIVE
IN ERASING PAINFUL MEMORIES SO THAT YOU CAN
THINK ONLY HAPPY THOUGHTS. USEFUL FOR
ERADICATING BOTH SHORT-TERM AND LONG-TERM
MEMORIES, EXTRANOL PREVENTS HARMFUL, NEGATIVE
THOUGHTS WHILE ALLOWING YOU TO REMEMBER WHAT YOU
MUST TO LIVE A HAPPY, HEALTHY LIFE. SAY GOODBYE TO
NIGHTMARES AND TRAUMA, BECAUSE LIFE IS TOO SHORT
NOT TO HAVE A BALL ON EXTRANOL!

HOW EXTRANOL WORKS

EXTRANOL USES POWERFUL BETA BLOCKERS THAT INTERFERE
WITH NOREPINEPHRINE AND EPINEPHRINE, KEY CHEMICAL
MESSENGERS THAT ARE RELATED TO THE STORAGE OF
NEGATIVE MEMORIES IN THE BRAIN. IN THIS WAY, EXTRANOL IS
ABLE TO INHIBIT THE CREATION OF NEW, ADVERSE MEMORIES
WHILE SIMULTANEOUSLY TARGETING AND DESTROYING PREVIOUS
UNFORTUNATE RECOLLECTIONS STORED IN DNA WITHOUT
IMPACTING THE BRAIN'S ABILITY TO CREATE
NEW POSITIVE MEMORIES.

DISCLAIMER

Extranol is a W.C.O.-approved controlled substance
and must be used with caution and under strict
medical supervision. Studies show that short-term
use of Extranol is safe and effective and may be
helpful in removing painful memories. Long-term use
may result in memory loss, brain damage, psychosis,
dementia, anxiety, and depression.

EXTRANOL

[May 5, 2035]

Got arrested today for killing a man. He deserved it. Life in the Restricted Zone is hard. You gotta fight to survive. Cha Cha Reynolds murdered my Pa. Said so himself. Told me to my face. So I picked up a bottle and smashed it over his head. Then he spat in my face and tried to scream for his boys to help him, but I snapped his neck. I watched as his eyes rolled back in his head, and his body went limp in my arms. Folks heard about it but didn't care much. Cha Cha owed most folks money. He lied his way around town. Made enemies of friends. Bragged too much, too. I still felt a little bad at first. But after thinking about it, I realized if I hadn't done it, he would have done it to someone else. We all gotta die sometime. I'm sure someone will do it to me one day, too. Only it's gonna take an army.

[May 28, 2035]

Got put in detention for two years. I don't care 'cause I was tired of living in the Restricted Zone. Detention is alright. They give you food. The other kids in here are too scared to mess with me. They do whatever I say. The psychologist let me try some new VIRTS on history. I learned that before zones there were neighborhoods and cities. And before the W.C.O., there were things called countries. People would fight when their countries disagreed. People seem to fight over anything. Nothing's really changed. We may change what we call things, but people are people just the same.

[August 3, 2035]

Killed a guard today and now I'm waiting to be sentenced. He tried to do things to me. Things I didn't want. I felt him touch me, and I punched him. I didn't mean to hurt him. Guess I hit him harder than I thought. He fell back, and his head busted open like a watermelon. They said he died quickly. I told them what he did, but I don't think they believed me. They ignored me. The prison psychologist wrote down what I said, and he says he's going to file a report. I don't think it's going to make any difference. The guards say I'm going to be transferred to a maximum security prison 'cause of my size and 'cause I'm a danger to the other juvenile inmates.

[February 14, 2036]

It's been a while since I wrote in this thing. Been in maximum security now for six months. Had my first fight to the death. The guards set up the barred fights, pitting two inmates against each other until one can't be beaten no more, cause he's half-dead or already there.

I like to fight. I'm bigger than most, so I don't mind it so much. I've never fought anyone and lost. Except my old man. But I was only twelve then, and he used to break people for The Constables, one of the toughest gangs in the Restricted Zone.

The guy I beat was a teenager with a squeaky voice and a narrow head. He had two different colored eyes, too. One was black the other, I swear, was bright red. Maybe it was scratched or bloodshot or something. It was hard not to look at. It distracted me at first. He even got the first few punches in 'cause I was too busy staring at his big, red eye. Then he made the mistake of getting close enough for me to punch him. I hit him right in the throat like my Pa taught me. Felt his bones crack.

He started squealing real fast. Started spitting up blood everywhere. He fell to the floor, clawing at his throat like he was trying to tear it open so he could breathe. I tried to stomp him out of his misery, but he kept flopping around, making it hard. Even the prison guards who normally like to watch our fights and place bets could hardly look. Eventually, I managed to step on his skull. He stopped squealing fast after that. Stopped doing much of anything. Seconds later, he was as cold and stiff as the prison bars.

[March 18, 2036]

Had another fight today. This time against one of the biggest guys in this place. The Executioner, they call him. Killed eight guys before fighting me. At first, I was nervous. I don't worry easily, but if you get enough people saying you should be scared, well, it's hard not to be. The guards all bet I wouldn't last a minute. So I decided I was going to hit him harder than I ever hit anything in my life. The guards were right. The fight didn't last a minute. The Executioner swung. I blocked it. Then I hit him square in the face with my fist. I don't think he bothered to block or duck. His whole face sunk in like a pancake, and he collapsed. His body started to convulse hard. He let out a giant poop while vomiting all over himself. Then he let out a deep gasp and died. Nobody said a word to me after that.

[April 1, 2036]

Today I was transferred to another cell. Dragon Matador is my new cellmate. Said he had me transferred. Said he has more power than the warden in this prison. Claims he rules much of the Restricted Zone from behind bars. I know he ain't lying 'cause I heard his name before. He heads one of the most powerful gangs in the Restricted Zone. The Matadors are vicious killers. Other than the Constables—who outnumber the Matadors at least three to one—no gang is stronger. But the Matadors are the most ferocious. If they want you dead, they'll make sure it happens. Then they'll kill anyone you like. Your mom, your dad, any siblings, even your neighbors, unless you happen to be neighbors with one of the Matadors. They make their money selling illegal ALTs to other zones. He said I had nothing to worry about as long as I worked for him and did what he said. I asked him, "What do you want me to do?" He said, "I want you to keep fighting for me." I told him I didn't mind fighting, and that I would.

[June 9, 2036]

Today I had to fight four men. It wasn't fair because they had pipes and knives, and I had nothing but my own two fists. Dragon had one of his men teach me boxing, karate, and wrestling. I've been training for months. That's why I haven't made any entries until now. That training paid off 'cause I beat these men badly. The fight lasted a while though so I'm glad I trained hard. I think it took a whole five minutes. I just grabbed one of the biggest guys and swung him around like he was my pipe, knocking the other guys down and smashing his skull against theirs'. I blocked their strikes with the guy's head and body. Eventually, all four of them were knocked unconscious. Then all I had to do was stomp them dead one by one. Dragon, my boss, was so happy, he told me he talked to the Warden, and they have a big surprise for me. I'll have to wait a few days to find out what it is.

[June 14, 2036]

Today, I got pulled into the doctor's office, and they told me they needed to extract some blood so they could clone me. I had to sign some paperwork agreeing to let them. Dragon said prisoners have the option to be cloned so their clones can work in the free world in order to pay off the prison sentences of their sources. Sources are what people who allow themselves to be cloned are called. I guess it's very common for prisoners to be cloned. They tattoo the clones blue so they can distinguish them from their sources.

[July 4, 2036]

Today, I got sent to the doctor's office again. These men in white suits injected me with something that made me sleep. When I woke, I was blue. Meanwhile, this other version of me sat on a chair in the corner of the room just staring at me with this blank look. Only his skin was as black as mine had been. I told them they must have made a mistake. They weren't supposed to make me a clone. But the men insisted there was no mistake. They said this was best. This way, I could go out into the free world while my clone remained behind bars. They said Dragon had it all arranged. He said I wasn't to tell nobody, or I'd be finished. I knew what that meant.

"What's your name?" I asked the clone. He replied, "Tumult." I had to laugh. "Yes, sir," I said, shaking my head. I never laugh. I think this really surprised the guards and the guys in the white coats. They kept looking at each other and looking back at me, and at my clone. They were really not sure what to do before escorting me out of the office.

As he was escorting me out, one of the guards said to me that I was one of the lucky ones. Normally, they use Extranol to erase a clone's memories so they have no trace of their former selves. They also undergo weeks of behavioral therapy to ensure that there isn't a single trace of leftover memories. "Why was I special?" I asked. The guard shrugged his shoulders.

As they led me through the prison, I noticed none of the prisoners were looking at me. It's like they were all told to look the other way. Next thing I knew, I was outside, being picked up by a limo. I was told someone working for my boss would be in touch with me. I was going to work for a very wealthy family who thought I was really a clone. They made it clear I was not to disappoint them.

The guard said that my boss was responsible for getting me out of prison. He said he could put me back just by just saying the word if I didn't continue to work for him on the outside. He asked me if I understood, and I said yes. "Basically, I may be free, but I'm still a slave," I told the guard. The guard grinned and patted me on the shoulder without saying a word.

[July 20, 2037]

It's been a year since my last entry. There's so much to write, I don't know where to start. After I got out of prison, I was taken by hovercraft to Astra and her family's mansion way out in the middle of nowhere. That's when I started working for Ophelia, Astra's Aunt. The job was simple: keep Astra safe. I drove her to all of her shows, always accompanied by Torin, Astra's butler, who has worked for the family for many years. But after nearly a year, Ophelia started to trust me, and I was finally left alone with Astra.

Astra was safe with me. She was a great person to work for. I don't think she has a mean bone in her body. From the start, she treated me with love and respect, as if I were her brother. She's what you call an Innocent, kept in an EMO-REG from the day she was born. I was never allowed to wear one of those things. I think it's because when you do, it's way too easy to become lazy. I protect Astra. That's my job. You can't do that when you're wearing an EMO-REG. Who's going to want to bust someone's head when they're feeling all blissed out?

A few weeks ago, this guy came to the house, supposedly to check on the security systems. Only he pulled me aside to whisper in my ear about how he works for my boss, and that I'm supposed to kidnap Astra and take her to Restricted Zone 69 where I had grown up. Once there, she would be held for ransom. I knew if I refused, my boss would report me to the law. Then I'd be back in prison where I'd probably be executed. Or I'd be assassinated one day on a routine drive into the free zones by someone just like that security service guy. Some guy posing as a regular member of society who, like me, worked for my boss.

Still, I've grown to love Astra. I'd rather die than betray her. Besides, if I were to do what my boss asks, there is really no telling what would happen to me after that. So a few days ago, I decided to risk everything and confess to Ophelia.

Let's just say that it would appear Ophelia has some powerful connections of her own. Of course, if you know Ophelia, that is obvious by the way people treat her everywhere she goes. I hoped that if I confessed in an effort to protect Astra and show my loyalty to her family, Ophelia would forgive me for having deceived her all these years. Otherwise, my backup plan was to escape into the desert and try my luck at surviving on my own—even though I knew I'd probably die in a few days. It was better to die though than to be sent back to prison after tasting the freedom I had those past few years working for Astra and Ophelia.

Fortunately, my plan worked. Ophelia made a few calls and worked out a deal with my boss. After that, I was told that I was a free man. I would never have to worry about working for my boss again. I could continue to work for her and Astra for as long as I wanted. If I didn't want to continue working for them, I was also free to leave. Nobody would be looking for me. I couldn't believe it. It took me months before it all sank in. For the first time in my life, I feel free.

5
HECTOR'S STAND

CHAPTER 5
HECTOR'S STAND

HELLO, HECTOR.

DESIRAE?
WHAT THE HELL IS GOING ON?!
I'LL SHOW YOU.
BUT NOT HERE.
VRROOOMMMMM

I HAD THIS PLACE.
BEFORE I LEFT YOUR BROTHER.
I'VE BEEN HERE BEFORE, HAVEN'T I?
MEMORIES LONG LOST...
...AN AFFAIR I'D FORGOTTEN.

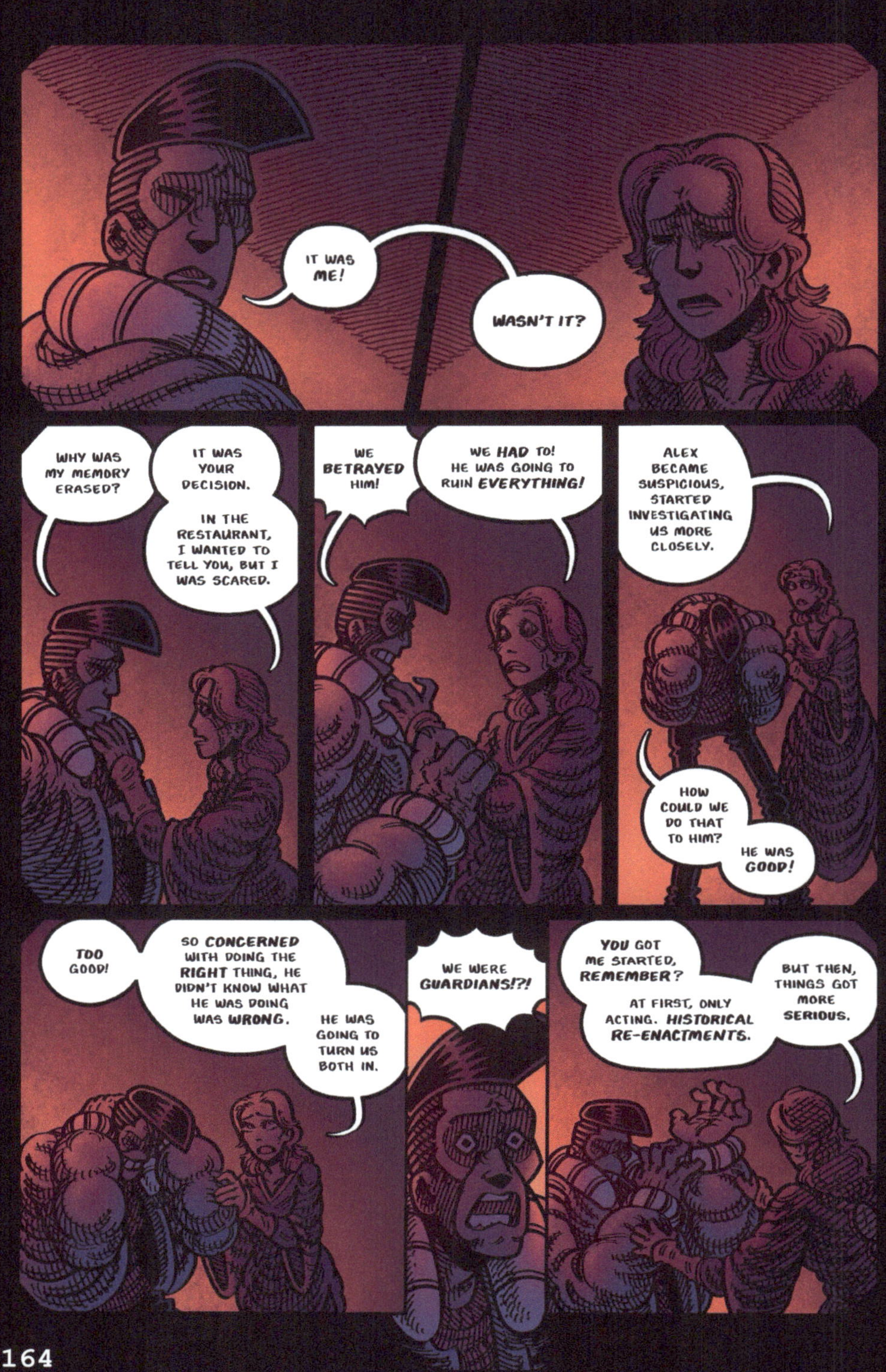

IT WAS ME!
WASN'T IT?
WHY WAS MY MEMORY ERASED?
IT WAS YOUR DECISION.
IN THE RESTAURANT, I WANTED TO TELL YOU, BUT I WAS SCARED.
WE BETRAYED HIM!
WE HAD TO! HE WAS GOING TO RUIN EVERYTHING!
ALEX BECAME SUSPICIOUS, STARTED INVESTIGATING US MORE CLOSELY.
HOW COULD WE DO THAT TO HIM? HE WAS GOOD!
TOO GOOD!
SO CONCERNED WITH DOING THE RIGHT THING, HE DIDN'T KNOW WHAT HE WAS DOING WAS WRONG.
HE WAS GOING TO TURN US BOTH IN.
WE WERE GUARDIANS!?!
YOU GOT ME STARTED, REMEMBER?
AT FIRST, ONLY ACTING. HISTORICAL RE-ENACTMENTS.
BUT THEN, THINGS GOT MORE SERIOUS.

YOU DON'T KNOW HOW HARD IT'S BEEN THESE PAST FEW YEARS, WITH YOU NOT REMEMBERING.
FORGOTTEN BY THE PERSON YOU CARE MORE ABOUT THAN ANYTHING ELSE IN THIS WORLD.
I BETRAYED HIM!
I BETRAYED A.R.I.S., TOO!
WE WERE IN LOVE!
ALEX REFUSED TO ACCEPT THAT --REFUSED TO SEE THE TRUTH.
HE WOULD RATHER US GO TO JAIL, THAN BE HAPPY TOGETHER.
HE WAS GOING TO DESTROY US! EVERYTHING WE STOOD FOR!
I LOVE YOU, HECTOR.
I'VE ALWAYS LOVED YOU.
AND YOU LOVED ME ONCE, TOO.
CRACK

HOW DID
THEY
FIND US?
DOESN'T
MATTER!
RUN!
ARIS
WHERE
ARE WE
GOING?
"TO GET
SOME
HELP."
STOP
STOP
STOP
STOP

K-CHK
YOU BETTER JUST OPEN THE GATE.

THE BLACK HOLE
HELLO, MATRIX.
HECTOR FRAKIN' HOLMES.

LET'S SAY HELLO TO MARVIN.
OOF!
SHALL WE?

MARVIN!

CHK
CHK
CHK
I HAD NOTHING TO DO WITH WHAT HAPPENED TO SAM!
CHK
CHK
CHK
I KNOW.
COCO TOLD ME ALL ABOUT IT.
WE CAN TAKE YOU TO THEM!
HELP YOU GET YOUR REVENGE!
YOU'D BETRAY THEM?!
IT'S NOT YOU I WANT.
I WANT THE GUARDIANS.
THEY'VE GONE TOO FAR.
THEY NEED TO BE STOPPED.
FOR SAM.

171

DON'T MOVE.
WHAT?
GRAB
IT'S A TRAP!

THVMM
THVMM
THVMM
THVMM
THVMM
FWMP
WAIT--
THUMP
THUMP

WELCOME BACK, HECTOR.

TMP
TMP

DONESTRE PAGAN.

YOU REMEMBER.

SIGH

BAM

HECTOR!
TWO YEARS EARLIER.
STAY OUT OF THIS!
ALEX.
YOU CAN'T ESCAPE.
THEY WON'T LET YOU.
DON'T YOU SEE?! WHAT YOU'RE DOING IS WRONG!

THE W.C.O. IS TRYING TO CONTROL US.
MAKE US FORGET, WHO WE ARE.
STEAL AWAY THE VERY EXPERIENCES THAT MAKE US HUMAN.
DON'T YOU SEE? WE CAN'T LET THAT HAPPEN!
SHUT UP!
ALEX. DON'T!
YOU TRAITOR!
DON'T BE A FOOL!
WE'VE GOT YOU SURROUNDED.
PLEASE, ALEX. JOIN US.
WHILE THERE'S STILL TIME.
NEVER!

NO!
YOU CAN ALL BURN IN HELL!
STOP!
IT DOESN'T HAVE TO BE THIS WAY.
WHAT OTHER CHOICE IS THERE?
YOU'LL ERASE MY MEMORIES?
FORGET EVERYTHING?!
SO MUCH PAIN!
NO.
I CAN'T.

ALEX
KILLED
HIMSELF.

BUT WE
DROVE HIM
TO IT!

I
REMEMBER
NOW.

ON THE
ROOF.

AMAZING.
YOUR MEMORY-- MORE RESILIENT THAN I EVER IMAGINED.
WE HAD TO STOP HIM.
HE WAS THREATENING THE REVOLUTION.
YOU MEAN YOUR REVOLUTION!
NO.
I MAY HAVE CREATED THE TECHNOLOGY, BUT YOU CONCEIVED THE MASTER PLAN.
YOU'RE THE HERO, HECTOR. YOU KEPT A.R.I.S. FROM SHUTTING US DOWN, WHILE WE GREW OUR FORCES, MUSTERED THE RESOURCES WE NEEDED.
TO HELP THE PEOPLE WAKE UP.
WHAT ABOUT THE PEOPLE IN HEAVEN'S HALL?
WE HAD TO GET OUR MESSAGE ACROSS. WHAT'S A FEW HUNDRED LIVES, WHEN THE W.C.O. WANTS TO CONTROL US ALL?

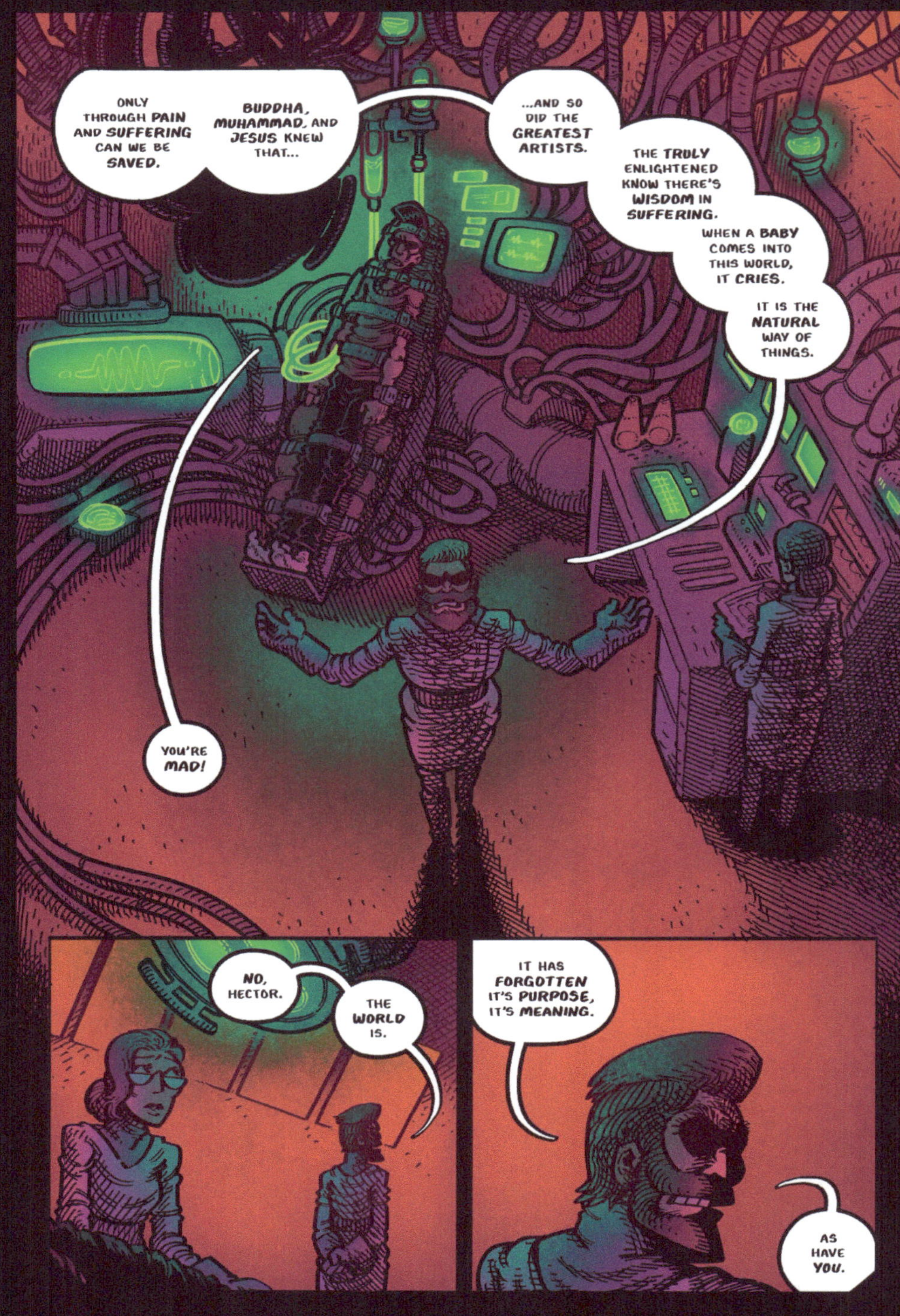
ONLY THROUGH PAIN AND SUFFERING CAN WE BE SAVED.
BUDDHA, MUHAMMAD, AND JESUS KNEW THAT...
...AND SO DID THE GREATEST ARTISTS.
THE TRULY ENLIGHTENED KNOW THERE'S WISDOM IN SUFFERING.
WHEN A BABY COMES INTO THIS WORLD, IT CRIES.
IT IS THE NATURAL WAY OF THINGS.
YOU'RE MAD!
NO, HECTOR.
THE WORLD IS.
IT HAS FORGOTTEN IT'S PURPOSE, IT'S MEANING.
AS HAVE YOU.

YOU'RE GOING TO SAVE THE REVOLUTION, HECTOR.
BY MAKING YOU A MARTYR.
BY KILLING ME?
A SAVIOR.
A GOD.
KER-
CHK

GOODBYE, HECTOR.
GOODBYE !!!
!!! MY FRIEND.

## DR. MOORE'S CONFIDENTIAL REPORT ON PATIENT HECTOR HOLMES – MARCH 3, 2050

Based on careful analysis and interpretation of Hector Holmes' experience and brain scans, along with in-person sessions, I have determined that Hector is suffering from bipolar disorder and demonstrates self-destructive behaviors.

Hector has a tendency to pursue painful, psychological experiences through the abuse of alternative reality drugs so as to avoid the emotional pain, which stems from the untimely death of his parents in a car accident when he was five years of age. This traumatic experience involved his whole family (which, at the time, included his parents Gideon and Frances, and his older brother Alex).

In the past, Hector has expressed jealousy for Alex, whom Hector claims physically and emotionally abused him for years, blaming Hector for the death of their parents.

Hector has a complicated relationship with his brother, who remains his only surviving family member. Hector has admitted to misusing the very same alternative reality drugs he has been tasked with monitoring and controlling as an A. R. I. S. agent. Furthermore, Hector has admitted to harboring guilt for involving himself in an affair with his brother's wife.

Hector is clever and displays a high degree of emotional intelligence at times. However, Hector's disdain for authority, his extreme mood swings, typical of bipolar disorder, and his self-destructive tendencies make him a possible danger to himself.

Today, Hector shared the details involving the death of his parents. Hector and Alex were in the backseat of the car while their father, Gideon, was driving and their mother, Frances, sat in the front passenger seat. According to Hector, the fatal accident was triggered by a fight between him and his brother over a pebble. Alex, then nine years of age, had found the pebble and claimed that it contained special powers, including the ability to grant a wish to anyone who held it. This resulted in an altercation in which Hector tried to retrieve the pebble from his brother. In the struggle, Hector bumped his father in the elbow, causing him to swerve and drive off the road.

Neither Hector nor Alex were wearing seatbelts, and they were ejected from the vehicle as it veered into an embankment, subsequently exploding and catching fire. Hector was rendered unconscious immediately after being tossed through the front windshield. Alex, who was also thrown through the front windshield, remained conscious long enough to witness their parents burn to death while still trapped inside the vehicle.

According to Hector, he had been the one who suggested that neither he nor Alex wear safety belts to prove that they were not scared of being hurt. Hector believes that his refusal to wear a safety belt may have resulted in saving both Hector and his brother Alex's life.

This incident seems to have contributed to Hector's habit of breaking the law and his overall disdain for authority.

Hector has reported being placed on probation by A. R. I. S. for violating several policies and procedures around criminal investigation. During previous sessions, Hector admitted to and even boasted about having deep connections with organized crime syndicates in the Restricted Zone. He explained that this was a result of his failure to comply with A. R. I. S. policy and his willingness to abuse his authority to serve his own addiction to Negative Alternative Experiences, known on the street as NEGs.

My recommendation is that my patient, Hector Holmes, continue to receive brain scans and cognitive behavioral therapy along with gene reversal therapy and prescriptive Extranol treatment to erase some of the painful memories that contribute to his self-harming behaviors. After treatment, patient should continue to undergo post-treatment evaluation for a period of thirty (30) days.

NUMBER:
FI450.22.30.01.00045A
DATE: 09.07.2053

DEAR DESrae,

THERE's no easy way for me to say this, so I guess I'll just come right out with it.

I know you are having an affair.

To say that I am devastated doesn't begin to express how I feel. It's hard to imagine a future in a world where I might have to live without you at my side, knowing you could hurt me as you have.

I realize I've been distant--probably too caught up in my work. Looking back now, I'm sure the long hours, missed dinners, and broken promises helped to push you away. I thought that my service to A.R.I.S. was making a difference. In my mind, I was helping to keep society safe!

You've begged me to tell you more about my work, and I didn't. I used the excuse that I was sworn to secrecy, but that's only partly true. I was also trying to protect you from the darkness of this world: people pawning off gruesome and twisted memories for all to experience as if they were an amusement park ride. You can't imagine the toll it takes on you to be confronted with the worst of humanity every day. I've had to harden myself to it. I built a wall around myself to keep it out. I never meant to keep you out too.

Though the W.C.O. does what it can to shield you from it, there's so much death, suffering and pain in the world. I've seen enough to know that it must be controlled before it drives us all mad! It may have been foolish, but I thought I could spare you from it if I kept you in the dark. Now it seems that my actions may have driven you to it.

You've told me many times that I close myself off to you and hold things in. I'll admit, it's true. Still, in my quiet, solitary moments, I KNOW that I am better for having you in my life. You've tried to HEAL ME WITH YOUR LOVE, and I appreciate it, Desirae, but some wounds run TOO DEEP.

A few weeks ago, I overheard you and Hector mocKING ME FOr being TOO serious and it hurt. Unfortunately, I had to groW UP FAST TO help raise Hector after our parents died. I often envied hIm FOR HIS Ability to embrace his desires and imperfections, but it was a luxuRY I DIDN'T have. My willingness to do whatever it takes to care FoR THOSE I love is what you once said most attRACTed you to me.

That's why I'm GOING TO RISK my life to warN YOU NOW: I suspect your "lover" is with the GuaRDIANS OF PAIN. I only HOPE HE HASN'T dragged you into it with him. The GuarDIANS OF PAIN AREN'T WHO YOU THINK THEY are! I realize their intentions may SEEM NOBLE, appEALING TO YOur liberal political sensibilities, but you don't KNOW WHAT'S Really ouT THERe: people illegally trading away the experienCES OF PRISONERS bEING EXECuted to make a profit; twisted individuals SELLING The suICIDAL RECollections of ex-lovers for some attenTION; MURDERErs aND PEDOPHILEs recording their victims' last dying memoRIES TO SATIsfy a sICK THRILL. WHAT the Guardians of Pain produce is no DIFFERENT. IT'S all part OF A DISEASE THat plagues our world, sewing DISORDER and decay, uNTIL SOON NO ONE WILL bE SAFe! I could show you the HoRRORs they've alrEADY INFLICted ON INNOCENT PEople, but there's no time.

Please take this as A FINAL WARning FROM SOMEONe who still cares foR YOU, despite everything. I BEG OF YOu, seVER All ACTIVITY WITH the GuardianS OF Pain before it's too laTE! SOON I will have enOUGH EVIDENCE to indict aND arrest anyone assocIATED WITh them. As much AS IT WILL DESTROy me IF I have to choose beTWEEN TAKING them down to savE THE WORLD AND MY LOVe for you, you know WHAT I WILL DO.

I'm sorry for eveRYTHing. I STILL CARE FOr you more thar YOU KNOW.

FOREVER Yours,

ALex

6
THE CRUCIFIXION

WHERE AM I?
THIS EXPERIENCE FEELS SO REAL.
TOO REAL.
ALL THE WORLD'S A STAGE.
INRI
CLENCH

RRIP
POP
THE PAST BECOMES THE PRESENT.
THIS IS NO MEMORY!
RRRAAAAAAHHHHH
FWMP

KILL
HIM!
HUFF
HUFF
RRAAAGH
THWACK

KRAK
KRK-K

SHUNK

STOP!
YOU'RE ALL UNDER ARREST!
ANYBODY MOVES, WE WILL OPEN FIRE.
RUN!
POP POP
POP POP

THUMM
THUMM

DESIRAE!

I'M SORRY.

ME, TOO.
KOFF
KOFF
POP
POP
POP

ARTEMIS CHECKED THE DNA.
YOU WERE RIGHT.
DONESTRE ISN'T DEAD!
THAT'S NOT ALL!
TORCH IS A LIE. IT'S ALL A SHOW!
THEY'RE USING REAL PEOPLE!
SLAM
VVVP
TARGET LOCKED!
VVVP

SHIT!
THEY'VE GOT US SIGHTED!
DUCK!
BOOM

MIKE!
YOU'LL LIVE. JUST STAY DOWN!

COVER YOUR FACES!
HEAD TO THE ESCAPE TUNNELS!
LONG LIVE THE REVOLU--
KRAK

ANOTHER STUDIO.
ANOTHER TRIP DOWN MEMORY LANE.
TITANIC
KRANK
SMACK
CLACK
CLACK

SNAP
UGH.
RRAAAGH!
THOKK
HVFF
HVFF
HVFF
DRIP
DRIP
SORRY, HECTOR.
YOU PUT ON A GOOD SHOW.
BUT YOUR ROLE'S ABOUT TO GET CUT.

SHNK
YYAAAAAAHHH!!
OOF
WHAM

I SEE THINGS DIFFERENTLY.
SPLKT
IT'S TIME YOU DID TOO!
KER-CHUNK
MELODY!

LET'S GO!
THROUGH HERE!
HURRY!
BEFORE THEY MAKE IT THROUGH THE DEFENSE SYSTEM!
ARE YOU HURT?
THAT'S FAR ENOUGH!
YOU WON'T WIN THIS FIGHT.

MELODY'S DEAD.
SIGH
USING eJUNKIES TO RE-ENACT TRAGIC SCENES FROM HISTORY-- PAWNING IT OFF AS TORCH!
THAT'S YOUR SOLUTION? CREATING FAKE MEMORIES?
KILLING PEOPLE?
eJUNKIES! ALREADY WASTING THEIR LIVES!
THIS WAY, THEY CAN DIE PROPHETS. MESSIAHS. GODS!
WAKING THE WORLD UP TO THE TRUTH!
DAMN, THESE RATS JUST KEEP COMING.
BANG
WHIZZZ
DOESN'T MATTER.
GUESS I'M THE EXTERMINATOR.

SLUMP
BUT THE BIGGEST RAT IS GETTING AWAY.
DONESTRE!

SHFF
KRAK
AAAHH!
I'M ENVIOUS.
THUD
CLATTER

YOUR ABILITY TO FEEL PAIN!
SNKT
GAHHH!
AND TO OVERCOME IT.
MY CONDITION ROBBED ME OF THAT HUMAN EXPERIENCE.
AAH!!
GO AHEAD.
I CAN TAKE IT.
SHNK

YES, YOU CAN.
IT'S THE EMOTIONAL PAIN YOU CAN'T FACE.
SH HK
GRAB
RRR!
CHNNK
SNAP

OOH, I BET THAT HURT.
HOW DO YOU STOP A MAN WHO FEELS NO PAIN?
I NEED TO FIND A BETTER WEAPON!

THERE'S
NO EXIT,
HECTOR.
I KNOW
YOU'RE
HERE.
YES...
...LET'S
FINISH
THIS.
SSSSST

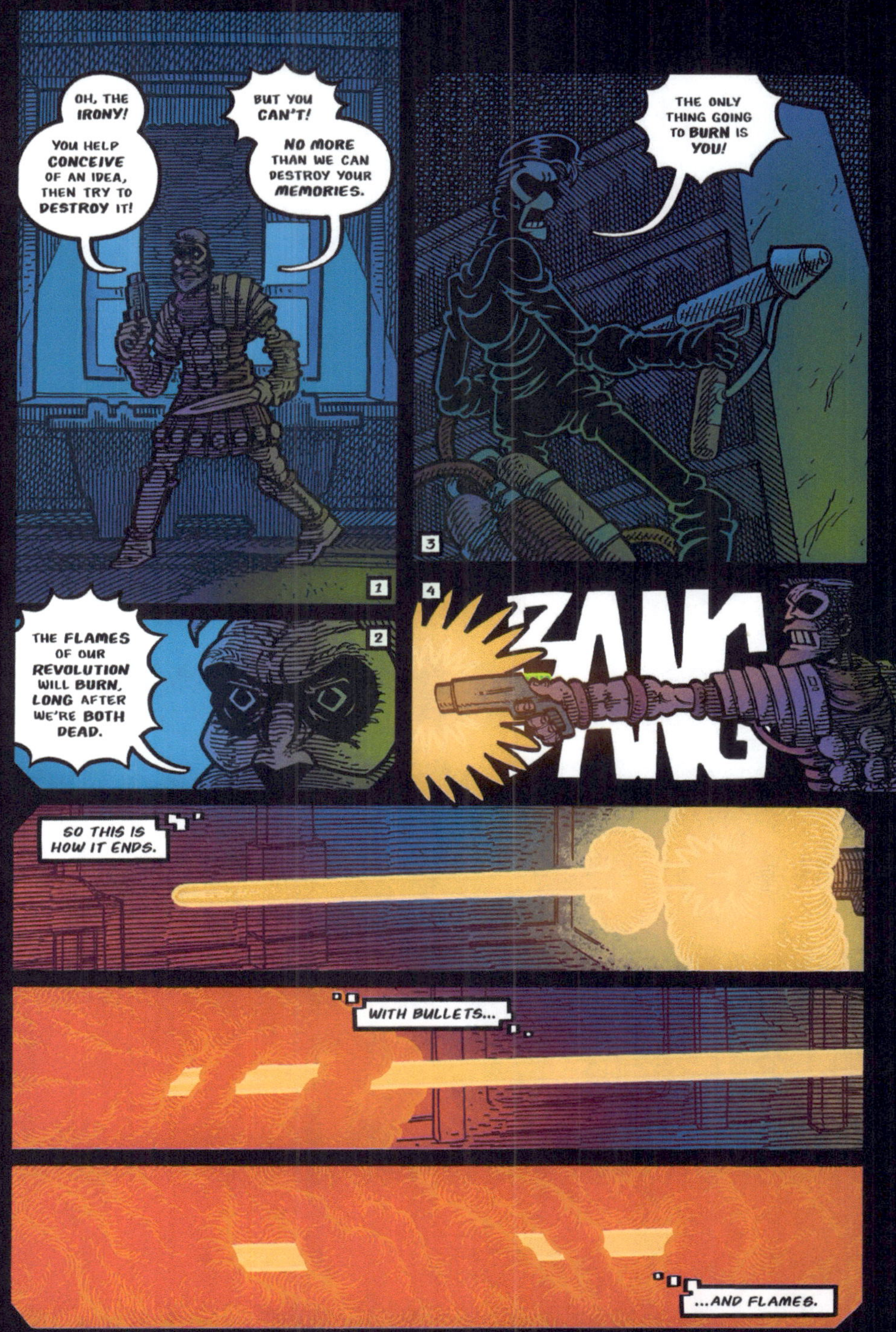

OH, THE IRONY!
YOU HELP CONCEIVE OF AN IDEA, THEN TRY TO DESTROY IT!
BUT YOU CAN'T!
NO MORE THAN WE CAN DESTROY YOUR MEMORIES.
THE ONLY THING GOING TO BURN IS YOU!
THE FLAMES OF OUR REVOLUTION WILL BURN, LONG AFTER WE'RE BOTH DEAD.
ZANG
SO THIS IS HOW IT ENDS.
WITH BULLETS...
...AND FLAMES.

CRACKLE
CRACKLE
THUD

GOODBYE,
DONESTRE.
THERE
HE IS!
MOVE
IN!

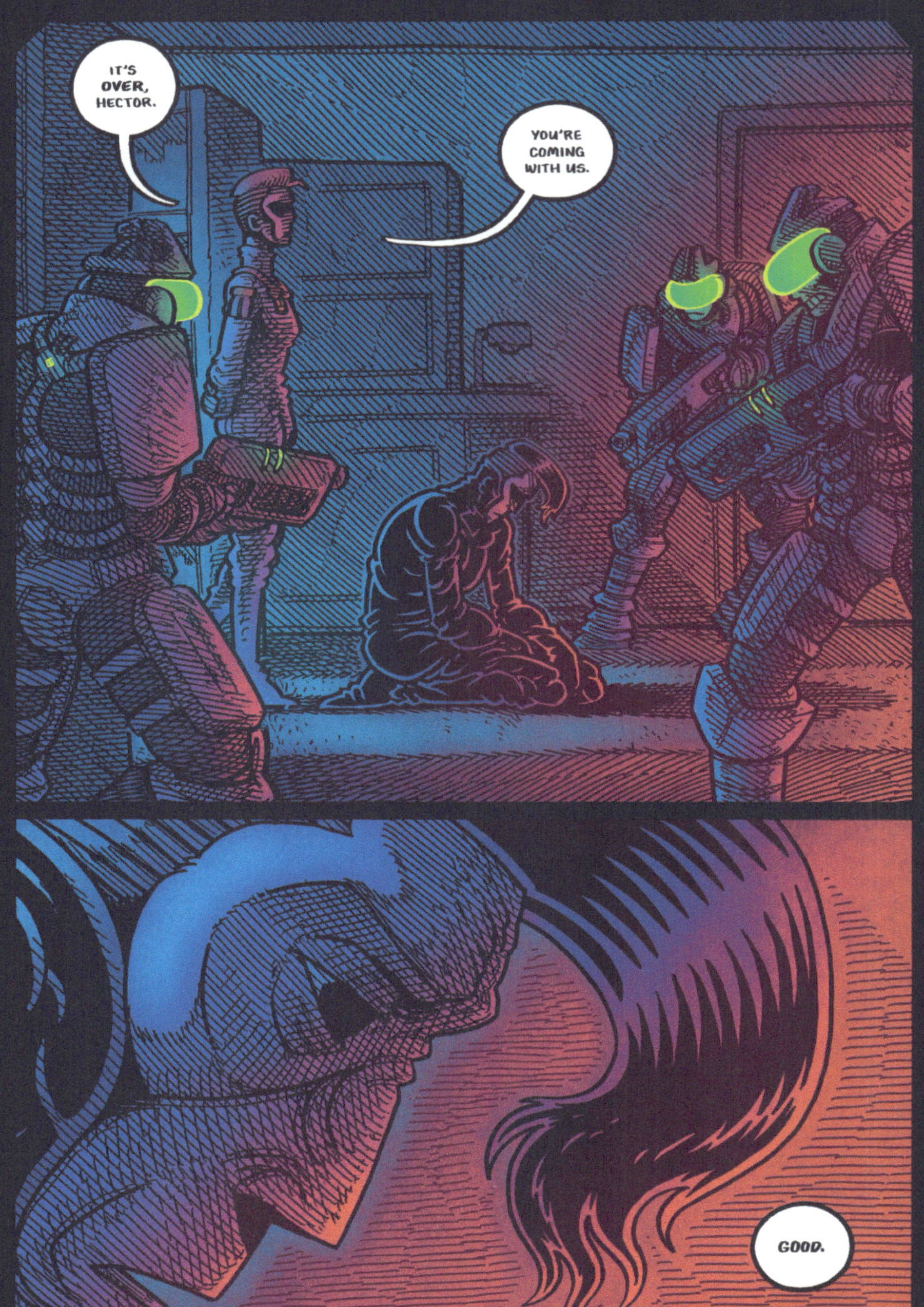

IT'S OVER, HECTOR.
YOU'RE COMING WITH US.
GOOD.

HECTOR 8119
HOLMES -32
HERO OR
VILLAIN?

GUARDIANS OF PAIN
LEADER DONESTRE
PAGAN DEAD IN
SHOOTOUT.
D-MORE


*BZZT* YOU HAVE A VISITOR.
AM I ALLOWED TO HAVE VISITORS?
IT'S BEEN APPROVED.


HECTOR?


HELLO, ASTRA.
YOU'RE NOT WEARING YOUR EMO-REG?
"THE TRUTH WILL SET YOU FREE."


MY TRUTH DESTROYED LIVES.
IT'S BETTER THIS WAY.
CHIRP
CHIRP

I'M WORKING WITH THE PEOPLE AGAINST TECHNOLOGY TO BLOCK THE LAW REQUIRING EMO-REGS.
THEY'RE ALSO TRYING TO HELP ME GET YOU OUT.
IT DOESN'T MATTER.
BUT IT DOES. YOU CHANGED MY LIFE.
SOME EXPERIENCES CAN NEVER BE FORGOTTEN.
I'LL NEVER FORGET YOU.
TIMES UP. FINISH YOUR CONVERSATION.
I'M SORRY.
ABOUT WHAT?
I HAVE TO GO.
BUT I'LL BE SEEING YOU, HECTOR HOLMES.
SEEING ME HOW?

KSSHHHT
IN MY DREAMS.
FLAP
FLAP
FLAP
FLAP
FLAP
FLAP
FLAP
FLAP
FLAP
FLAP
FLAP
FLAP
FLAP

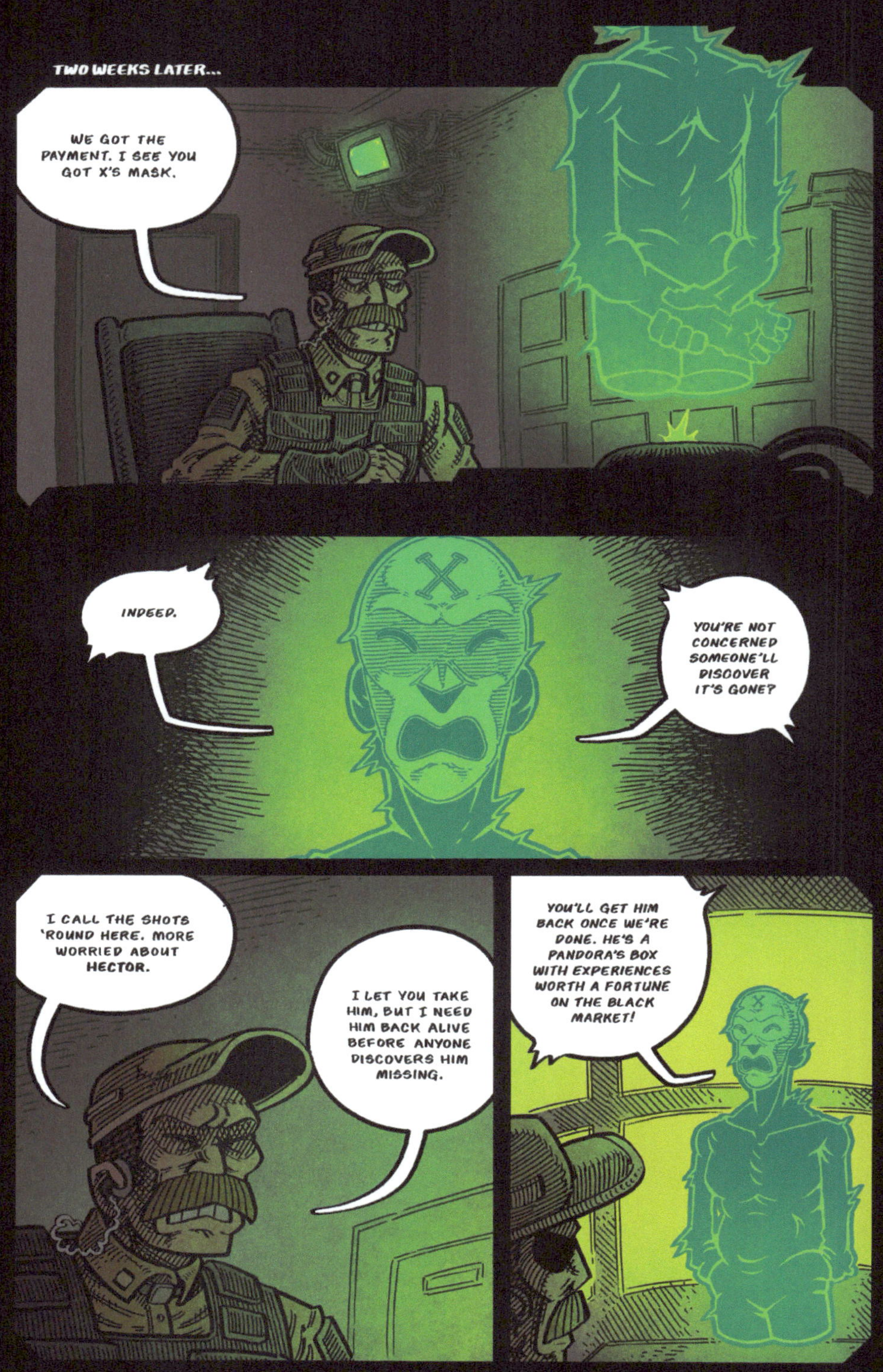

TWO WEEKS LATER...
WE GOT THE PAYMENT. I SEE YOU GOT X'S MASK.
INDEED.
YOU'RE NOT CONCERNED SOMEONE'LL DISCOVER IT'S GONE?
I CALL THE SHOTS 'ROUND HERE. MORE WORRIED ABOUT HECTOR.
I LET YOU TAKE HIM, BUT I NEED HIM BACK ALIVE BEFORE ANYONE DISCOVERS HIM MISSING.
YOU'LL GET HIM BACK ONCE WE'RE DONE. HE'S A PANDORA'S BOX WITH EXPERIENCES WORTH A FORTUNE ON THE BLACK MARKET!

SO YOU CAN SELL BOTH THE PROBLEM AND THE SOLUTION.
EVERY HERO NEEDS A VILLAIN AND VICE VERSA. KEEPS YOU IN BUSINESS TOO, WARDEN.
WARDEN
UNTIL NEXT TIME...
CLICK
SMASH

DON'T TRY TO BREAK FREE, HECTOR.
RESISTANCE IS FUTILE.
BESIDES, YOU WON'T REMEMBER ANY OF THIS.
NOT THIS TIME.
NOW, RELAX!

THE END.

## "THE RISE AND FALL OF PARADISE LOST STUDIOS"
### BUSTER CHAPLIN

Paradise Lost, once a famous movie studio, now languishes away in Zone 999, home to an industrial cluster of warehouses and factories.

The gradual decline of the acting profession and the movies they produced began decades ago with the collapse of unions, the shift away from traditional media advertising, and advancements in technology that led to a flattening of the entertainment industry. Eventually, digital avatars of historical figures and actors long dead came to replace real ones.

What followed was the fusion of movies and rock concerts with virtually shared experiences. Documentaries and books were soon replaced with virtual historical reenactments. Then new technology appeared that would dramatically change the landscape of entertainment once more.

The invention of Nerve Reading Devices opened up a new world of sharing dreams—literally! The streaming of dream projections created an economy of dreamscapes with dream celebrities as the stars, resulting in a whole new expression of Carl Jung's concept of the collective unconsciousness. People started to grow obsessed with the transparency of hopes, dreams, and feelings.

Enter nanotechnology, and what is called Alternative Reality. No longer were people limited to fabricated, virtual simulations. With Alternative Reality, everyone could relive past experiences as if they were happening in the present. Or dive into the cellular memory of others. Glorydazing became a huge trend in which people could relive their high school romances ad infinitum.

Our lives are now driven more by Alternative Reality experiences than by our own individual ones. As emotional regulation and Alternative Reality continue to capture a larger share of an evolving market, the demand for AR threatens the few studios that remain.

The association of Paradise Lost with Donestre Pagan and The Guardians of Pain has brought down the final curtain on one of the last Virtual Reality studios to remain. Frankly stated, many wondered how they were able to survive this long.

Financed by Donestre Pagan, founder of Pagan Inc., and run by his brother, Christian Pagan, a renowned executive, the studio managed to survive for years. However, recent events have unveiled a tragic reality. Most of the actors employed by the studio were secretly involved in historical reenactments used to create the Alternative Reality drug known as Torch.

Mike Miller, the A.R.I.S. agent who cracked the case, said in an interview with The Free Press, "Donestre wanted a place to recruit the actors working for the studio. He convinced them to participate in historical reenactments that would be recorded and pawned off as real Alternative Reality experiences to be sold as Torch."

He and The Guardians of Pain believed that pain and suffering were necessary for human survival and that the W.C.O.'s recent efforts to regulate those emotions would result in their own demise. The pitch appealed to the egos of actors who felt insignificant in a society that no longer valued what they had to offer. Instead, Donestre, pretending to be the respected studio executive, offered each of these actors the role of a lifetime, a chance to be heroes in the fight to stop the evil empire, the W.C.O.

Himself willing to die to advance his ideology, Donestre now had an extended family imbued with religious fervor and willing to do whatever it took to kickstart the revolution.

However, as demand for Torch grew, The Guardians of Pain needed to supplement their supply of martyrs willing to die for the cause with eJunkies who would do anything for a fix, even if it meant losing their lives. The studio continued to create historical reenactments, only this time, they were not used to make Virtual Reality schlock that few cared to buy—but to create a new form of Alternative Reality.

The recent A.R.I.S. raid on the studio and the death of Donestre Pagan put the final nail in the coffin of The Guardians' efforts and tarnished the legacy of another bankrupt studio. All that remains is the memory of glory days long past… and a name befitting its demise.

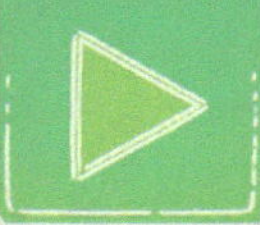

INVESTIGATIVE REPORT STATEMENT -- A333.45.607

I began my investigation of former A.R.I.S. agent Hector Holmes on September 9, 2053, after he reported having witnessed his brother, Alex Holmes, commit suicide by jumping from the roof of the warehouse building located at Restricted Zone 69, 780 Hollywood Blvd. There were no other witnesses at the scene of the alleged suicide. This made Hector a prime suspect in an investigation into the events leading up to his brother's death, as there was no evidence in Alex's routine A.R.I.S. psych evaluations that suggested suicidal ideation. I recommended to A.R.I.S. and to police officers investigating the case that a full murder investigation be initiated, but my request was denied.

Alex Holmes had been deeply involved with an ongoing investigation into The Guardians of Pain, and as indicated above, routine emotional testing revealed no warning signs that he may be suicidal. In addition, I had spoken with Alex on a number of occasions, and he confided in me that he had some concerns for his safety. These concerns were based on the sheer power and reach of The Guardians, and the recent alliances they had made with many of the more dangerous gangs working in Restricted Zone 69.

Hector reported that his brother appeared to be under mental duress but reported no knowledge as to why Alex may have committed suicide. According to Hector, no words were exchanged between them as Alex leaped to his death.

Memory scraping of Hector Holmes corroborated his written statement. Based on available evidence, Alex Holmes' death was ruled a suicide, and the case was officially closed.

A note retrieved from Alex's home, written to his wife, Desirae Holmes, did indicate that Alex was suspicious his wife was having an affair with someone involved with The Guardians of Pain.

Hector's statements were called into question by my superiors given his employment history, prompting further investigation. Hector had acquired an extensive knowledge of memory hacking and cellmem scraping during his time as an Alternative Reality Investigator. His employment was terminated after it was determined that he was guilty of tampering with evidence and abusing ALTs while on the job. However, because of several incidents in which he was asked to use highly addictive Alternative Reality drugs while working as an A.R.I.S. agent in the Restricted Zone, his violations were pardoned, provided that he sought therapy.

A week after Alex's death, Hector was assigned to psychiatrist Dr. Moore. Investigations into Dr. Moore's notes later revealed that Hector had been the one having an affair with Alex's wife Desirae. Several years after Hector was assigned to psychiatric treatment, Dr. Moore was investigated for her association with The Guardians and her assistance in manufacturing Torch.

During this time, her notes on Hector were pulled and evidence of his affair with Desirae was uncovered. Additional notes led me to believe that it is possible Dr. Moore was the person who introduced Hector to The Guardians of Pain and that Hector may have later introduced Desirae to the group.

During my investigations into Hector's activities, he was found to be entering Restricted Zone 69 on a weekly basis to purchase illegal Alternative Reality Drugs. As a result of this revelation, my investigations continued.

On October 23, 2055, Hector was admitted to Sun Valley Hospital on Bellview and Straighter in Zone 9 and was reported by doctors to be in a coma but recovering. Traces of the drug Torch were found in his blood. I met with Hector on October 25 after he woke up. During this time, I proposed that Hector work with A.R.I.S. to investigate The Guardians of Pain. However, I indicated clearly that his work would be unofficial since, given his dismissal, he would never be allowed to work for A.R.I.S. in an official capacity again. During this conversation, I indicated that A.R.I.S. had uncovered evidence linking Desirae to an affair with a member of The Guardians. Though at the time, I had no solid evidence that Hector was affiliated with The Guardians, I did have evidence linking him to the affair with Desirae. Hector had little interest in helping with my investigation. However, he did appear surprised to learn that Desirae had been having an affair. Over the course of our conversation, I indicated that he had been tracked illegally entering Restricted Zone 69. Hector asked if I was going to have him arrested. I avoided giving him a direct response but did indicate that had I wanted to arrest him, I would have done that already. Shortly after that meeting, Hector's Ad Apparel, which we had been using to track him, was discarded in the trash near his home.

A few weeks later, on the intersection between Catalina and 8th St., Hector was found unconscious. He reported that he had witnessed the abduction of several eJunkies by people dressed like The Guardians. He reported that he had been drugged and rendered unconscious by one of the masked Guardians and that they had called him by his name. At that time, Hector also indicated that he would like to help with the investigations.

During the next few weeks, further evidence linking Hector and Dr. Moore corroborated my suspicions that Hector had been deeply involved with The Guardians. However, it was clear from my conversations with Hector that he had no recollection of his involvement. In fact, he was investigating The Guardians of Pain himself to better understand his own possible ties to the organization. His escape from A.R.I.S. allowed us to track him to The Guardians of Pain's headquarters located at Paradise Lost Studios on November 25, 2055. See my full report of the incident here: [A333.45.608].

Memory scraping of Hector after his recovery at Paradise Lost Studios led to powerful evidence identifying Donestre Pagan as the leader of The Guardians of Pain. Hector's previous investigations regarding Donestre Pagan's corpse helped us make a giant break in the case and led to the eventual arrest and or elimination of many of the group's core members.

**ADDITIONAL COMMENTARY**

It is the opinion of this agent that Hector Holmes should be pardoned for his previous crimes, having no recollection of them, and for his heroic effort to bring down The Guardians of Pain. His addiction to Alternative Reality drugs began while he was working for A.R.I.S., and his ability to tolerate painful Alternative Reality experiences led to the recovery of much of his previous memory, which had been tampered with through the use of Extranol. His experiences continue to provide us with key information on members of The Guardians of Pain today.

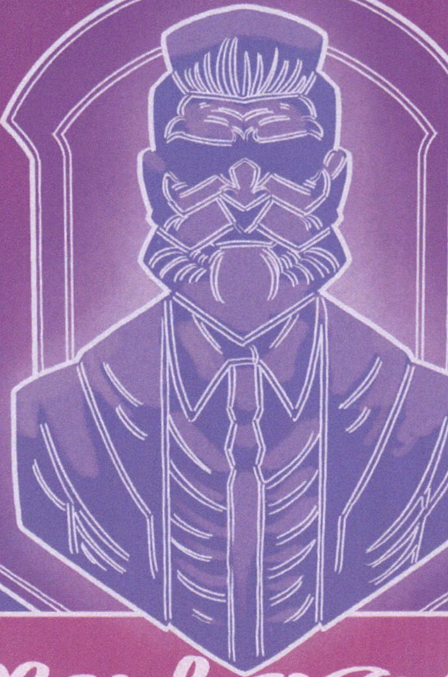

# Eulogy for Donestre Pagan

## Hero or Villain? Madman or Genius?

**Written by Dr. Emory C. Goldstein**

On October 20, 2055, Dr. Donestre Pagan died in a confrontation with A.R.I.S. All that remains is a legacy and infamy that will leave people with mixed emotions about who he was as a person. As his former professor and an academic colleague who worked closely with him on some of his key findings in DNA scraping, I feel compelled to set the record straight. Tragically, my humble musings will likely provide the only eulogy anyone will be bold enough to write for him.

Donestre was a remarkable student. He possessed a profound mastery of the subjects discussed and had the ability to see beyond conventional wisdom. His piercing insights shattered the limitations of existing theories with mind-boggling astuteness and a bold, iconoclastic willingness to reject all to get to the truth.

It was this that made him more than a brilliant student but a welcomed colleague. Unfortunately, his creativity, which allowed him to make connections between disparate proofs, and his tenacity to work until finding answers also allowed him to practice bad science. Regrettably, he did, on occasion, manipulate data to serve his own desired outcomes. When his advanced theories on DNA scraping of century-old corpses proved to be an impractical failure, he decided to cheat the process. Sadly, he fabricated an alternative reality drug that in truth was like any other, only that it was born of murder and suicide.

I'll spare the details on how this happened since plenty has already been reported and explained. What I want to offer are some reflections on his motivations so you can decide for yourself who he was and why he mattered.

At a young age, Donestre witnessed his parents die. They were burned in a house fire. Though he was suspected of having murdered them, there was no proof. New investigations may turn up novel evidence, but as of now, he remains innocent of this crime. Donestre had a twin by the name of Christian. After the death of their parents, Donestre and Christian were adopted by the scientist Bertrand Pagan. This scientist made his fortune developing sensors that would later be adopted in the Nerve Reading Devices that Donestre would come to invent when he created his own successful company, Pagan Inc., honoring the family name of his adopted father for years to come.

Donestre excelled in science and showed his adopted father's aptitude for invention and design. His brother, Christian Pagan, displayed a genius of his own but in the arts. He went on to become the executive head of one of the most powerful movie studios, Paradise Lost. His success was in part the result of his brother's financial power, as Donestre often financed many of Paradise Lost's biggest productions, allowing the studio to remain in business long after most of the other studios dissolved.

Donestre was also unique, not only for his genius but for a rare genetic disorder known as CIPA, Congenital Insensitivity to Pain and Anhidrosis. People with CIPA cannot feel pain, and most do not live to adulthood as a result. Further evidence of Donestre's intelligence and his instinct for survival can be seen in his ability to adapt to this condition and flourish despite the odds. His condition no doubt inspired his later obsession with pain. He valued it all the more because he himself could not feel it. As for suffering, he knew much of this since his condition and the superiority of his intellect resulted in his inability to form lasting relationships for years. It wasn't until late adolescence, observing his brother Christian, who was known as a charismatic individual, that he studied acting and taught himself to pose as the extrovert his true, introverted self despised. How he managed to pull this off enough to convince an army of actors and colleagues in science that he was Christian Pagan is still a wonder... both scary and impressive.

As time went on, Donestre went on to get his doctorate and co-authored a few papers with me. He left academia and research to start his own company, using the capital he inherited from his parents, while his brother used his portion to invest in and build Paradise Lost studios. Because Donestre's genius led to his creation of Nerve Reading Devices (N.R.D.s), he had the capital he needed to invest in nanotechnology, creating the drug Extranol, which would later make him billions. The drug is still widely used to treat severe depression and anxiety, though recently its side effects have caused many to prohibit its use except in extreme cases.

After the success of Extranol, Donestre became increasingly paranoid and irritable. He started to believe the World Corporation Organization was trying to use Extranol to control people, replacing their memories with ones of their own choosing. He thought the W.C.O. wanted him dead, convinced its leaders were plotting to take control of his company and the drug.

This resulted in Donestre going off the grid for a while. During this period, he became a founding financier and member of the group The People Against Technology (P.A.T.). Eventually, a split between him and senior leadership caused him to leave the group and form his own known as The Guardians of Pain. Donestre, much like those who co-founded P.A.T., believed the W.C.O. is trying to control people by manipulating their emotions through technological means. They are convinced that eventually machines will replace most humans and the economy would collapse, leaving only a few high-level executives in charge, much like feudal lords of medieval times.

The better part of Donestre wanted to stop this from happening. However, unlike P.A.T., Donestre believed that fighting the power of the W.C.O. without the use of technology is futile. Therefore, he used his genius and efforts to create a band of obsessive defenders he called The Guardians of Pain. These were people who would join in the fight and work to stop the W.C.O. no matter the cost. He found powerful allies using money from the sale of Pagan Inc. to finance his ventures, convincing people at high levels of society, even members of A.R.I.S., to support his efforts.

As his obsession with developing his theories on DNA scraping all failed, his frustrated efforts led to his plot to take over his brother's studio. In this way, he intended to fake what he was unable to build, at least until he could raise enough money to make his revolutionary vision a reality. The rest is history, with his obsessive efforts eventually leading to the murder of his own brother. Furthermore, he is undeniably responsible for the murder of countless, nameless eJunkies who unwittingly participated in his holy war against the powers that be. All of this was done in service of the effort to stop the mandate on emotional regulation no matter what the cost.

The recent deaths of people using EMO-REGs and the ensuing protests have caused many people to take P.A.T.'s message to heart and reconsider the mandate of emotional regulation in most of the zones. We will have to wait to see if Donestre Pagan's revolutionary message has a hand in how things evolve. Regardless of the outcome, few should doubt Donestre's genius or madness. As for whether he was a hero or villain, I'd venture to say it may be possible he was both, but only time will tell.

One thing is certain, despite his death, Dr. Donestre Pagan remains very much alive in the many ways he has changed the world.

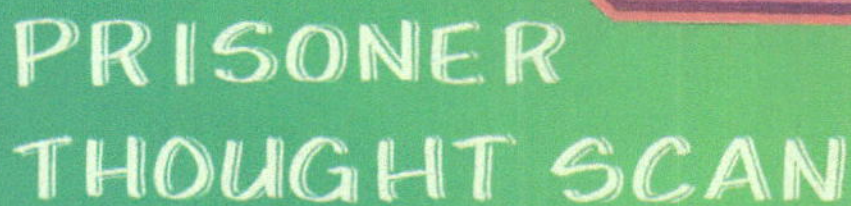

PRISONER
THOUGHT SCAN
LOG: PTSL40000000056
SUBJECT: HECTOR HOLMES



SUBJECT'S STREAM OF CONSCIOUSNESS HAS BEEN REVIEWED TO INCLUDE ONLY
THOSE THOUGHTS DEEMED A SECURITY RISK OR OF INTEREST TO THE PSYCHIATRIC
TEAMS. ALL RANDOM THOUGHTS CONSIDERED HARMLESS HAVE BEEN REDACTED.
REFLEXIVE THOUGHTS IDENTIFYING EMOTIONS WERE ALSO REMOVED UNLESS
EMOTIONAL REGULATION OR THOUGHT BLOCKERS WERE REQUIRED. THE FOLLOWING
EXCERPT WAS FLAGGED AS WORTHY OF ANALYSIS:



I'M WHAT YOU CALL AN EXPERIENCE JUNKY.
eJUNKY FOR SHORT.
WE DREAM OF EXPERIENCING EVERYTHING.
PLEASURE...PAIN...EVEN DEATH.
UNTIL THE DREAM...
BECOMES A NIGHTMARE.
IN SPITE OF IT...WHILE MOST PEOPLE ACCEPT
MANUFACTURED BLISS THROUGH EMOTIONAL REGULATION...
AN eJUNKY MUST EXPERIENCE IT ALL, NO MATTER THE COST.
MY EXPERIENCES BLEND TOGETHER.
NOT SURE WHAT'S MINE...WHAT'S SOMEONE ELSE'S.
THOUGHTS. FEELINGS. JUMBLED. TIMELESS.



[EMO-REGULATION ACTIVATED]



A WISE PERSON ONCE SAID:
"THOUGH THE FRUIT OF EXPERIENCE IS TASTY
TO LIVE A THOUSAND LIVES HAS CONSEQUENCES."
WHO SAID THAT?

[EMO-REGULATION ACTIVATED]

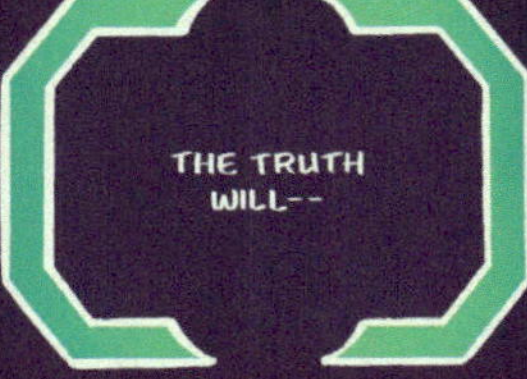
IDEAS.
WHERE DO THEY COME FROM?
DO WE REALLY EVER KNOW?
THERE'S WISDOM IN--

[SECURITY BLOCK ACTIVATED]

THE TRUTH
WILL--

[SECURITY BLOCK ACTIVATED]

WHY...CAN'T...I...
REMEMBER?
WHO AM I?
WHERE AM I?

[EMO-REGULATION ACTIVATED]
[INSERT HAPPY THOUGHTS]

I AM SAFE.
I AM LOVED.
I AM AT PEACE.

EARLIEST SKETCHES
OF HECTOR HOLMES

EARLY CONCEPT
FOR ASTRA

HECTOR W/
AD APPAREL

## THE GUARDIANS OF PAIN

MY ORIGINAL DESIGNS FOR THE GUARDIANS WERE A LOT MORE ORNATE THAN THEY LOOK IN THE FINAL VERSION.

I FELT A MORE MINIMAL DESIGN WOULD FIT BETTER IN A FUTURISTIC SETTING.

## W.C.O. ENFORCER

THE ENFORCER'S UNIFORM CAME TOGETHER PRETTY QUICKLY, AND DIDN'T CHANGE MUCH THROUGHOUT THE DEVELOPMENT.

THEY WERE AT LEAST PARTIALLY INSPIRED BY JIN-ROH: THE WOLF BRIGADE.

## FASHION STUDIES

WHEN DECIDING ON A FASHION STYLE FOR THE WORLD OF eJUNKY, I TRIED TO FOCUS ON BREAKING FORMS AND CREATING INHUMAN SILHOUETTES.

I WANTED THEIR FASHION TO BE AN EXTENSION OF THE TRANSHUMANIST PHILOSOPHY THAT IS A LONG-STANDING CORNERSTONE OF CYBERPUNK MEDIA.

INT. HOVER CRAFT - NIGHT

Hector opens his eyes, seeing his hands cuffed in his lap. He glances over to see Astra cuffed next to him. She stares, catatonically. Her once untarnished face now stained with tears, dirt and bruises.

A Guardian in a SCARED FACE mask holds a gun while leaning against the opposite side of the hover van.

Across from Scared Face kneels Happy Face, filling a syringe with a fluorescent green vial labeled "Extranol".

Happy Face sets the vial down, then turns to Hector with the syringe.

Hector smacks Happy Face's hand, which sends the syringe flying.

Scared Face points the gun at Hector.

Hector uses his cuffed hands to choke Happy Face from behind, using him as a shield.

> HECTOR
> Don't! Or I'll kill him!

Scared Face hesitates, then takes aim.

Hector shoves Happy Face into Scared Face.

The gun drops, firing.

Scared Face tries to recover it, but Astra kicks it toward Hector.

Hector grabs the gun and tugs open the back door.

Happy Face lunges for him.

Hector jumps aside and Happy Face tumbles out the back of the craft going into a nasty roll on pavement.

Hector points the gun at Scared Face, who backs away with both hands up.

> HECTOR (CONT'D)
> Against the wall!

Hector turns his attention to SERIOUS FACE at the wheel.

> HECTOR (CONT'D)
> Faster!

He presses the gun against the driver's head.

> HECTOR (CONT'D)
> I said go faster!

Serious Face speeds up.

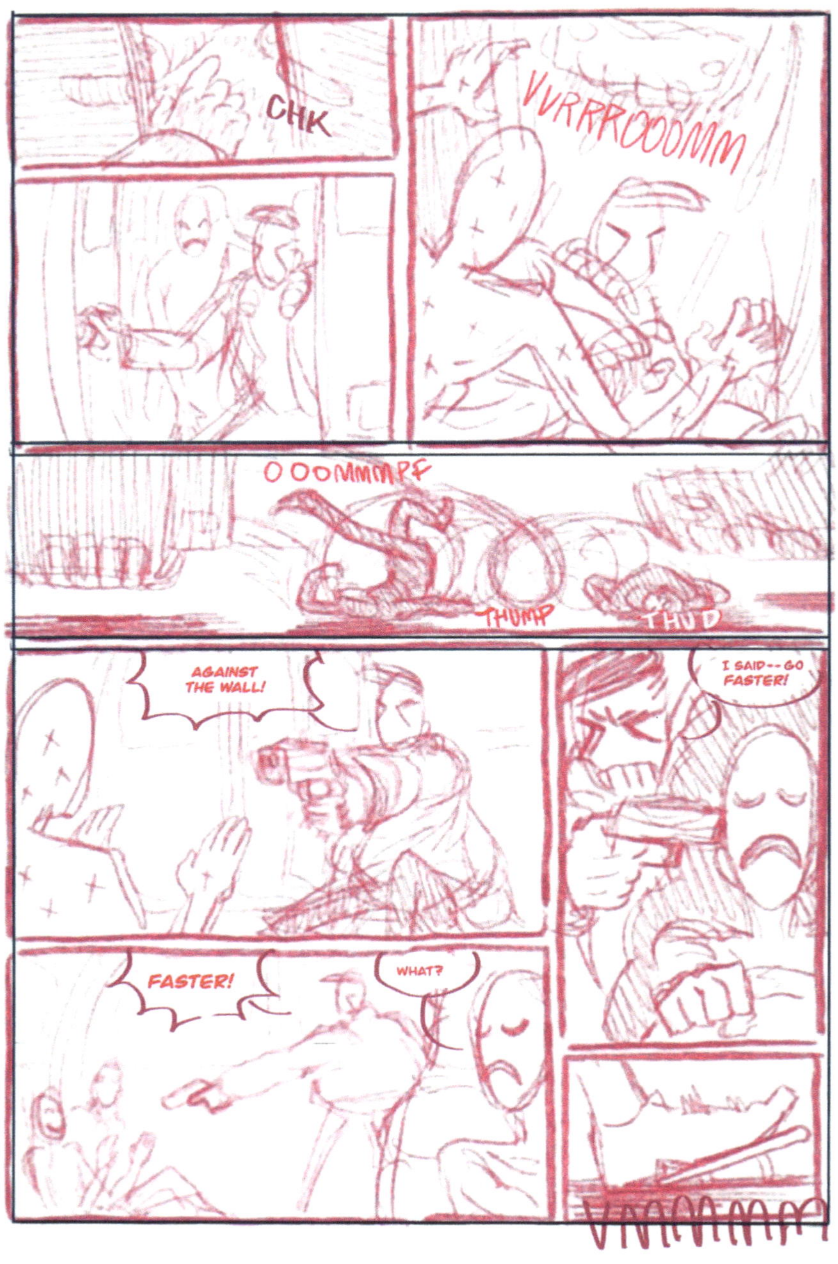


## THE SKETCH

I TRY TO KEEP MY SKETCHES VERY LOOSE, JUST SLIGHTLY CLEANED UP THUMBNAILS. I THINK THIS FORCES MORE ON-THE-FLY CREATIVITY IN THE INKING STAGE, WHICH LEADS TO MORE INTERESTING RESULTS.

IT ALSO MAKES THINGS MORE EXCITING FOR ME, RATHER THAN JUST TRACING WHAT I ALREADY PLANNED OUT, I NEED TO BE ACTIVELY ENGAGED IN THE PROCESS.

## THE INKS

INKING HAS ALWAYS BEEN THE MOST FUN PART OF THE PROCESS FOR ME. IT WAS ALMOST A SHAME TO PUT COLORS OVER THE INKED PAGES, BUT LUCKILY THE COLORING STYLE WE LANDED ON CONSISTED MOSTLY OF FLAT COLORS AND SMOOTH GRADIENTS, WHICH HOPEFULLY DIDN'T DISTRACT TOO MUCH FROM ALL THE WORK I PUT INTO THE HATCHING.

# ALTERNATIVE COVERS

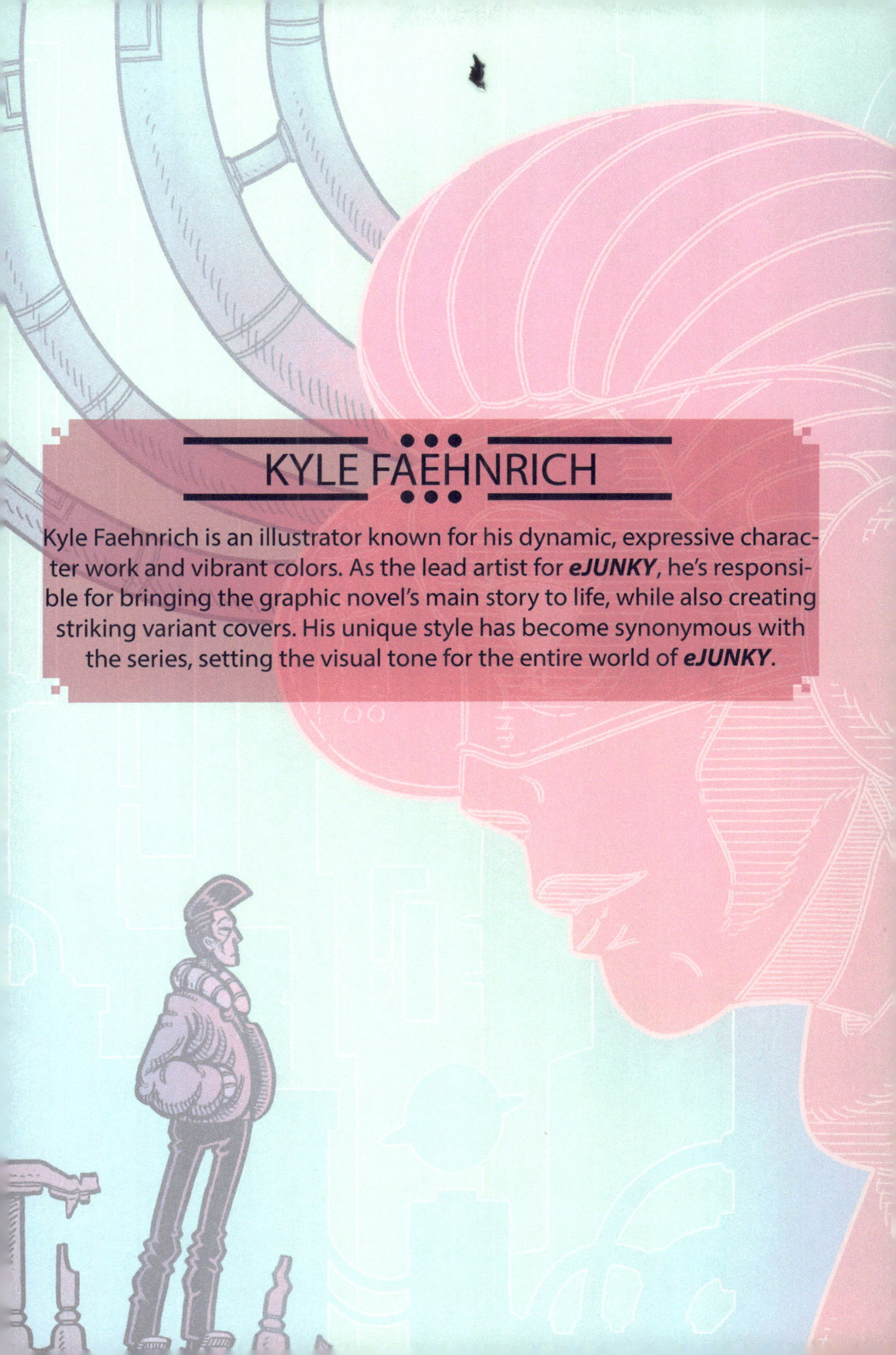
KYLE FAEHNRICH

Kyle Faehnrich is an illustrator known for his dynamic, expressive character work and vibrant colors. As the lead artist for *eJUNKY*, he's responsible for bringing the graphic novel's main story to life, while also creating striking variant covers. His unique style has become synonymous with the series, setting the visual tone for the entire world of *eJUNKY*.

# DANIELE SERRA

Daniele Serra is an Italian illustrator and painter with a distinctive, atmospheric style that often blends macabre themes with a beautiful, dream-like quality. Winner of the **British Fantasy Award**, his work is highly sought after in the horror genre and has been featured on numerous book and comic covers. For ***eJUNKY***, he lends his haunting artistic vision to a retailer incentive variant cover for issue #1.

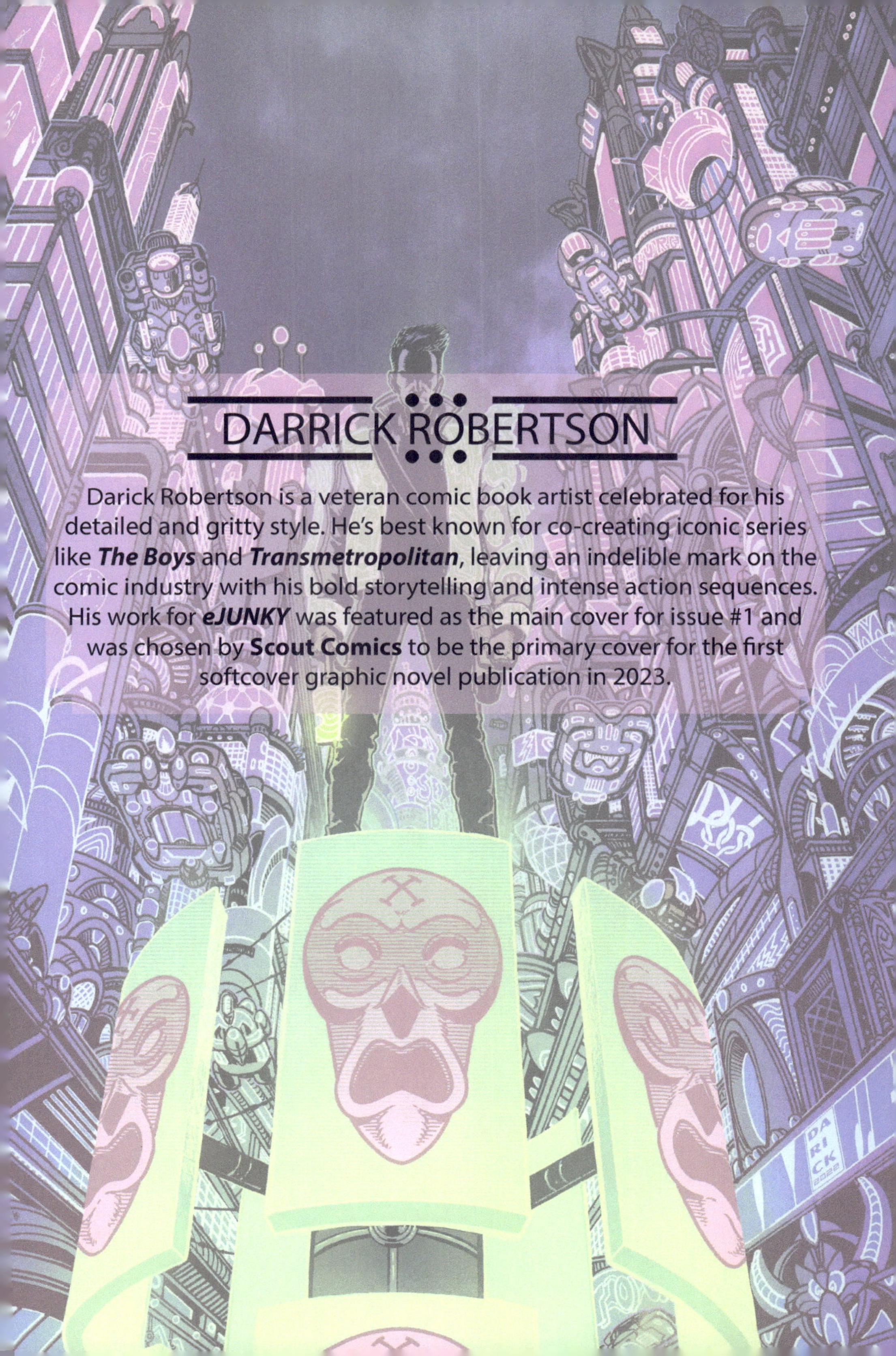

DARRICK ROBERTSON

Darick Robertson is a veteran comic book artist celebrated for his detailed and gritty style. He's best known for co-creating iconic series like *The Boys* and *Transmetropolitan*, leaving an indelible mark on the comic industry with his bold storytelling and intense action sequences. His work for *eJUNKY* was featured as the main cover for issue #1 and was chosen by **Scout Comics** to be the primary cover for the first softcover graphic novel publication in 2023.

# STEFANO CARDOSELLI

Stefano Cardoselli is a prolific Italian comic book creator whose art is defined by its kinetic, high-energy line work and cyberpunk-inspired aesthetic. Known for his creator-owned works like *DNW* and *The Outsiders*, he brings a raw, explosive quality to his illustrations. His contribution to the *eJUNKY* series is an alternative cover for issue #2.

THE
END[?]